Kate
the
Great

Winner Takes All

Suzy Becker

CROWN
NEW YORK

A little PRONUNCIATION KEY:

Mrs. Verlangen — ver·LANG·in

Verdi — meow.

Kate — VAIR·dee

Copyright © 2016 by Suzy Becker

All rights reserved. Published in the United States by Crown Books for Young Readers, an imprint of Random House Children's Books, a division of Penguin Random House LLC, New York.

Crown and the colophon are registered trademarks of Penguin Random House LLC.

Visit us on the Web! randomhousekids.com

Educators and librarians, for a variety of teaching tools, visit us at RHTeachersLibrarians.com

Library of Congress Cataloging-in-Publication Data
Names: Becker, Suzy, author.
Title: Kate the great : winner takes all / Suzy Becker.
Other titles: Winner takes all
Description: First Edition. | New York : Crown Books for Young Readers, [2016] | Series: Kate the great ; book 2 | Summary: "Armed with her smarts, an artillery of doodles, and maybe even some advice from Eleanor Roosevelt, Kate must find a way to keep her friends, old and new"—Provided by publisher.
Identifiers: LCCN 2015035040 | ISBN 978-0-385-38880-1 (hc) | ISBN 978-0-385-38881-8 (glb) | ISBN 978-0-385-38882-5 (epub)
Subjects: | CYAC: Friendship—Fiction. | Drawing—Fiction.
Classification: LCC PZ7.B3817174 Kaw 2016 | DDC [Fic]—dc23

Printed in the United States of America
10 9 8 7 6 5 4 3 2 1
First Edition

For my ★★★★★ niece Hildy
and my great niece Stella

WHUBAT NUBOW?

"No fair!" I am racing Fern to the front door and I fall. Baby sisters should *not* be allowed to answer the door unless they 100% know who is on the other side.

"Happy Fall On Your Behind Day, Kate!" my dad says as he steps over me to open the door. It's the first Sunday morning in November, the one when you set the clocks back. And that was my dad's idea of a joke.

EVERYONE* LAUGHS
(and their ages)

Fern
(4 yrs.)

Brooke
(10 yrs.)

Mrs. J.
(~~30~~ 40?)

Dad
(41)

* Everyone except ME, the Pope, etc., etc.
(10 yrs.) (80?)

Brooke's mom stops laughing and her eyes bug out when she looks at her watch. "I forgot the time change—I'm sorry, Adam! We can go and come back . . ."

"Seriously, we're early?!" Brooke says. "Intergalactic breaking news! My mom is early!!!" I pull Brooke into the house and up to my room before her mom can take her away.

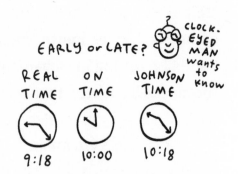

Brooke helps herself to my unmade bed and I get in beside her. "We have 39 minutes until Nora gets here," she says. Nora is our new, as in not even one month old, best friend.

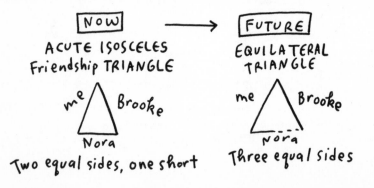

Before we were friends, my dad said, "There is a word to describe Nora." (He's a writer.)

I guessed, "Annoying."

CORRECT ANSWER →

Nora?

con·trar·i·an
Someone who always takes the opposite side

Once you get to know Nora, you realize she's not actually "taking" a side—it's just who she is. And, even though being friends wasn't exactly my idea, she really has grown on me. And Brooke. A lot.

The friendship was my mom's idea

Full story here!

"Thirty-*eight* minutes," Brooke says. "What do you want to do?"

"I better get dressed," I say.

"Ooh, sounds super-fun." Brooke pushes me out of bed. "Let's watch *America's Funniest Home Videos*. We can turn it off when Nora gets here." (Nora does not like AFHV.)

"Sorry, no-electronics Sunday," I say, which is why I usually try to go to other people's houses on Sundays.

"Then let's do our nails." Brooke throws her legs over the side of the bunk and sits up. (Nora doesn't like doing her nails—she says the polish suffocates them.)

I go down the hall to get the nail stuff. My sister Robin is in the bathroom with the door shut, which is a synonym for "privacy, please." It's perfectly silent in there, so I knock. "Are you going to be long?"

Find your answer in
The COMPLETE GUIDE to
TEENAGER BATHROOM ACTIVITIES

Not LONG

Just going to the BATHROOM

MEDIUM-LONG

working on zit, hair, OR makeup

FOREVER

(or BOTH or ALL THREE)

"I'll let you know when I'm out."

"Could you just hand me the nail polish bag?" Brooke and I are running out of alone-time. "Please?" The door opens enough for me to take the bag. "Thanks, Rob!"

Brooke still has yellow and white nails from her Halloween fried-egg costume. "I think I want copper," Brooke says.

The copper is Robin's, and I have recently, uh, taken ∧ some̶h̶o̶r̶s̶e̶thing
and returned
that was Robin's without asking, which is not an experience I care to repeat, so I run back to the bathroom.

Let's WEIGH the OPTIONS:

"DON'T ASK (she won't notice)"

ASK

WHAT NOW, KATE?

Yikes! "WHAT is on your face?!"

"Avocado and egg white."

I'll ask *why* later. "Can Brooke use your copper nail polish?"

"You can use any of my nail polish. Just make sure you put the lids on tight." *NEWS FLASH: I'm TEN, not TWO.* "Want some?" Robin waves a popsicle stick full of gunk at me.

"No thanks!" I say, racing to my room.

Brooke and I do our nails with the ceiling fan on, because I'm pretty sure nail polish fumes *can* suffocate you. My dad yells up, "Nora's here!"

"I'll put the polish away," Brooke says.

"And make my bed look—"

"*Make my bed, PLEASE, Ol' Buddy, Ol' Pal, Ol' BFF of mine,*" Brooke says.

"Right!" I go greet Nora. "My room's kind of a mess."

"Shocker!" Nora says in her sarcastic Australian accent. (I thought it was British before she corrected me.) "Wow, your room's actually *neater* than normal—the bed's made. Your dad said Brooke was here but I knew she couldn't possibly be—she's always late."

"I HEARD THAT!" Brooke jumps into the room with green gunk all over her face. I burst out laughing. Of course Brooke is also laughing, and when one of us is laughing it makes the other one laugh harder . . . until I notice that Nora looks like she might start crying, which is the ONLY scientifically-proven way to get me to stop laughing.

THINGS that WILL NOT
GET ME to STOP LAUGHING:

1. Asking me to explain why I'm laughing
2. Making me leave the room
3. Getting mad at me
4. Drinking water

"So what's the plan?" Nora asks.

"No plan. We were just waiting for you," I answer.

"Phew," she says. "Let's play Backwards 8ball."

♡ writing
↳ BACKWARDS ↙
8 BALL! ↖
↑
looks
the SAME

ACTUAL K8 BALL ANSWER
↳ "Yes, definitely!" ↲

"I have to wash this stuff off first," Brooke says.

The three of us made up a game with the "K8" ball Robin gave me for my birthday. Basically, whoever has the ball turns it over and reads the answer. Then the person who goes next has to come up with the question.

I hand Nora the ball. "Signs point to yes," Nora reads.

Brooke's turn: "Does Colin like Kate?"

"Does Colin *love* Kate?" Nora says.

"Signs point to you're both—" I make the cuckoo sign and whistle the cuckoo whistle.

Nora hands the ball to Brooke. Brooke reads, "Concentrate and ask again."

"Dubo yubou spubeak ububbi dububbi?" (Two seconds fake concentration.) "Sorry, do you speak ubbi dubbi?"

"It's easy," Brooke explains to Nora. "You just add 'ub' in front of the vowels. It used to be Kate's mom and dad's secret language."

"Lubet mube truby." We give her four thumbs up.

"My turn. 'Without a doubt.'" I look at Nora.

She looks down and says, "Am I moving to California?"

I drop the ball.

Brooke says, "What?" even though she heard perfectly clearly.

When you drop the K8 Ball, it...

A) bounces
B) cracks
C) shatters
D) rolls on

"You are not!" I say, even though she obviously is.

"My dad's been transferred."

"But I thought he was working in Hong Kong," Brooke says.

"After he gets back. We're moving at the end of December." Now we're all staring at the floor. What else is there to say?

"Well, if you *have* to move, California *is* kind of a cool place," Brooke tries. "Okay, that sounded really stupid, because California is literally a warm place, but . . . Will you be near Disneyland?"

"An hour and a half away. First thing my mom told me, like that would make up for ruining my life. Can we please not talk about it?"

Just then, like her wish was the Universe's command, my mom calls, "Anybody ready for lunch?" And we manage not to talk about It for the rest of the afternoon.

THE BRAID TRAIN

BIG LiTTle SISTER

It's getting close to dinnertime and my mom is

LOOK INNOCENT with:

Robin's FACEMASK
———————
AVOCADO
EGG WHITE
mash avocado.
Mix in egg white.

talking to the refrigerator door. "What happened to ALL my eggs?" I look at Robin. Robin looks at me and raises her eyebrows like they were never covered in egg-ocado.

"What do you need eggs for?" my dad asks. "Want me to run*out and get some?"

* Take the CAR. It'll be faster!

SCORE!
25,000 points for using Dad's joke on him!

"I was thinking breakfast for dinner." Mom shuts the fridge. "Recalculating . . . ," she says, imitating the GPS lady's voice. "We'll have dinner for dinner."

"Dinner for dinner—I like it!" my dad says. "I'm going to throw Fernie in the tub."

TOP 3 MEALS
PIZZA
PESTO PASTA
PASTA PESTO

My mom makes pesto pasta. "Look, snow!" Fern says. She is hogging the Parmesan cheese, as usual.

"Let's keep the snow *on* the pasta," Mom says, and passes me the cheese. "Everything okay with you girls this afternoon? Lunch was awfully quiet."

"Nora's moving," I announce. My mom and dad look guilty. "Wait, you knew?!"

"Her mother told me on Halloween night."

"Mom, I HATE it when you don't tell me stuff." My mom hates it when I say "hate."

"Nora wanted to tell you herself, but she didn't want to ruin your birthday. Or Halloween."

"Instead she's ruining Christmas."

"Christmas is a couple months away. Imagine how Nora feels, Kate." *Again?* I thought the part where

I had to imagine what it felt like being Nora all the time was finally over. "Maybe a new beginning will be good for Nora."

"Well . . . ," my dad says, reaching for Bob. (Bob is excellent at changing the subject.) "I believe we are talking about ladybugs tonight. Right, Fern?" Fern is big on putting bugs in Bob.

The Big Ol' Bowl of Conversation Starters
"BOB"
aka Our Centerpiece
DIRECTIONS: Pick a paper "starter" out of Bob. Discuss the next night.

Last night's pick

Fern nods and says, "Ladybugs are good luck!" which is good news, considering last Thursday afternoon there were about six hundred of them crawling around our upstairs bathroom window.

"I found out their knees bleed when they feel threatened," I say.

"Ew, gross, Kate." Robin makes a face, then continues in her super-grown-up voice, "When I

Bee's knees bandages

(magnified 800x)

was your age, Fern, someone told me that you could tell a ladybug's age by the number of spots on her back."

Reminder:
That was
ELEVEN,
not III,
years ago.

She makes a buzzer noise. "FALSE! So I've counted hundreds of teeny-tiny spots for no reason."

"Not so fast—the spots can tell you which ladybug you're looking at—there are a hundred and fifty different kinds. And"—sometimes I think Mom should've been a scientist instead of a lawyer— "technically, ladybugs are beetles, not bugs— they were originally called ladybird beetles. They *are* good luck, Fernie, for farmers, anyway—because they eat bugs, thousands in their lifetime."

"Lady Bird" Johnson's famous advice (for ladybugs & others):

Get so wrapped up in something that you forget to be afraid.

Wife of 36th President Lyndon B. Johnson

"Very cute, for cannibals!" my dad says, and Mom gives him The Eyebrows. "Your mother is trying to make my knees bleed. Want to pick a new one, Ladybird?" He holds the bowl out to Fern, and she hands him a paper. "Ahh, Coach Marden. He used to post this on our soccer team bulletin board every year."

> Winners know that every rule in the book can be broken except one — be who you are, and become all you were meant to be, which is the only winning game.
> — Sydney Harris

"That's technically two rules," I say.

"The rule is 'be who you are.' 'Become all you were meant to be' is the game," Robin says.

"Well, we have another rule around here." Mom crumples her napkin, which is a synonym for "dinner's over." "It's somebody's bedtime. . . ."

Fern raises her pesto-y hand. "Me."

Note to Self
Bathe child
AFTER
dinner.

"I'll do the dishes, Dad, if you want to take Fern up," Robin offers.

BROWN BEAR, BROWN BEAR, WHAT DO YOU SEE?

I see a guilty egg-face sister looking at me.

Rocky hears our chair sounds and comes running. (Rocky is a rescue dog, which is supposed to explain why he is always hungry.)

RULE #2 Rocky is no_t allowed to have people food.

RULE #2 Rocky i_s allowed to prewash the dishes.

I help Robin clear the table. "Sorry about Nora," Robin says. She turns the dishwasher on and sits down next to me at the table.

"It's not your fault."

"You must be a little relieved, though," she says. I might have agreed a month ago, but things are different now. Sometime back in the middle of October, being Nora's friend stopped being a project— not that it's regular (nothing's exactly regular with

Nora). Now I sit with her on the bus every day, both ways.

"Hey, thanks for not saying anything about the eggs." Robin pauses, and I half smile (no teeth). "I was wondering if you could keep another secret."

"Like what?" (I ♥ guessing games.) "You turned Fritzy's bark collar up to nine after you took him out this afternoon. No, wait—you put chili powder in the dryer with Dad's underwear—"

FRITZY
The Neighbor's Lean Mean
Nonstop Barking Machine

"Not something you or Brooke would do, Kate. Never mind, I was thinking now that you're ten you could be more like a *big* little sister."

"I can. . . ."

"I have a crush on Will." Will is her BFF Grace's older brother. Robin and Grace are training for the Thanksgiving Gobble Wobble road race.

ROBIN
with goo-goo dreamy eyes
in the warm citrus-breezy air...
(DISHWASHER SCENT)

"Will has been running with us. Please don't say anything to Mom and Dad; I don't feel like dealing with a hundred thousand questions and they would probably notice how I'm always over there—I know they mean to be supportive, but you know . . ."

Not exactly, but I pretend to know or else I would turn back into a *little* little sister. "Yeah. That's exciting!" I say big little sister–like and hug her. "I think I'm going to go to bed now. Don't worry. I WILL not tell—"

"KA-ATE!!!"

"Seriously, I won't. I swear."

I stay for an extra minute before I hug Robin good night, breathing in the citrus breeze.

SISTERLY LOVE

HOLY MACARENA

"TGIM, huh, Kate?" Gene says as I climb the bus stairs. *Translation:* Thank goodness it's Monday.

I say, "Right, Gene!" instead of my usual "Hi, Gene!" Then I slide in beside Nora, and he flaps the doors shut. Nora and I are quiet. I know she doesn't want to talk about moving, and the only other news I have is Robin's crush.

I actually think of another subject, but I'm not sure I want to bring it up with Nora. "Tomorrow is my ear-piercing day—not at the mall, at my doctor's."

"Good, because at the mall—"

"I know. The phone case guy's forehead." Her mom works at the mall, and Nora has already told me a hundred Piercing Pagoda horror stories, which have not helped my nervousness.

"It was his eyebrow. Swear you won't tell anyone." My swear is still good from the last time, but my pinky goes up automatically when it hears the word "swear."

"That's all right," Nora says. "I believe you." (She doesn't believe in pinky-swears.) We're quiet again. I hear her mumble something toward the window. Then she turns to me. "I said, do you want me to go with you, but you probably already asked Brooke."

"No—I mean, yes, I would, except you can't. Nobody can. It's a doctor's office. But thank you . . . so much . . . for asking."

TEMPORARY

TAKEOVER
by polite ALIEN

"Somebody took her polite pills this morning."

"I know." We both laugh. "But I really *do* wish you and Brooke could come."

Brooke is waiting for us in the bus circle. "Okay, want me to tell you, or want to be surprised?" she asks.

Brooke whispers in my ear, "Today's special is going to be *very* special. Mrs. Staughton's subbing. I saw her go in."

Nora says, "That's not a surprise. Mr. Mac is always absent the first day of gymnastics."

SUPER-observer NORA

When we get to gym (today's "special"), Mrs. Staughton is fighting with the music player. (You can see her through the door-window.) "Kate," she says as we walk in, "I'm going to ask you to be my assistant."

FALSE!! If you were going to Ask me, I could say NO.

"Sit right here, and when I give you the signal, please press play."

I get to sit on the pile of gym mats directly behind Mrs. Staughton. (Everyone else has to sit on the floor.)

"At this point in the year, I don't think I need to introduce myself and my fanny pack, but I'm going to anyway. I'm Mrs. Staughton. Mr. Mac is out sick today, so I have the pleasure of introducing your new unit. A unit that combines agility, strength, timing, grace, and humiliation."

I liked it a lot better before Mrs. Staughton became our Junior Guide leader, when she was just some substitute with a freaky fanny pack. Hui Zong and Eliza are the only ones still looking at her. "Anyone care to guess?" No one cares to guess because everyone already *knows*.

Finally Eliza raises her hand. "Gymnastics."

"Gymnastics and _____?" Now we're all stumped. "Gymnastics and dance, which is also known as rhythmic gymnastics."

Mrs. S. divides us into our "performance teams." Thomas, Brooke, me, and . . . Mrs. S. is about to announce our fourth.

"Colin Smith."

Thomas whispers, "Yesss!" I stare extremely hard at my shoelaces. Nobody, especially not Colin Smith, needs to see my red face right now.

"Okay, everybody up! Let's start with one we all know!" Mrs. S. signals to me. "Hit it, Kate."

The "Macarena" starts blasting.

By the time the song ends, Mrs. S.'s fanny pack has pushed her sweatpants down, and the top of her underwear is showing. "Did you notice—she tucks her shirt into them," Brooke points out on the way back to 5B. I barely smile.

↖ *no pun intended**

"Oh, c'mon, what's wrong? Isn't this your dream team? You wanted to be Colin's partner for the colony—"

"Shhhh! I don't want Colin to hear."

"You get to *dance* with him!"

"Him *and* you *and* Thomas, in front of the whole class. *That* is a nightmare!"

* REMINDER
I do NOT
like puns.

25

"No, *this* is a nightmare!" Brooke pulls her underwear waistband up over her shirt and folds her arms. I have to laugh.

Reasons why Brooke is my Best Friend:

13. She can make me laugh even when I really don't feel like it.

Brooke calls me after dinner.

"I don't actually have anything to say. It's just the last time I'll get to talk to your unpierced ears, you know, on the phone."

"I'm a little nervous," I admit.

"Well, it's just like a shot, two shots, but you get earrings—" She hesitates. "I'm kind of making it up. I had mine done when I was a baby. See, it can't be *that* bad, or they wouldn't do it to babies. . . ."

"Thanks. See you tomorrow?" We hang up and I reach for my K8 ball.

TWO HOLES in MY HEAD

"Oww!"

"Kate, Dr. Churchill only made a red dot on your ear with a Sharpie," Mom says.

How embarrassing. I am glad I am not at the mall. On a Saturday. With a thousand people watching.

I AM usually BRAVE.
i'm not afraid of ① SHOTS or the ② DARK.
③ i try NEW foods.
④ I don't cry when I get hurt.

"All right, Kate, now you might feel a little pinch—"

"Do you mean like a shot, or like—"

"Like . . . that!" Dr. Churchill rolls her chair back. I give her

REMINDER
Get so wrapped up in something that you forget to be afraid.

a thumbs-up. "And that!"

BRAVE
(continued) ⑤ I don't cry when I get my ears pierced.

"All set! Happy belated birthday!" Dr. Churchill hands me my ear-care instructions.

I glance down at them and ask, "So I should probably skip gym for the first few weeks, just to be on the safe side. . . ."

Dr. Churchill winks at my mother. "You can resume all normal activity—just keep your ears clean."

Like I said...

"You look so grown up, Kate. I can remember

RHYTHMIC
GYMNASTICS ≠ NORMAL
ACTIVITY

bringing you into this office when you weighed just six pounds," Mom says.

MY EARLIEST MEMORY
"Feeding a goat." Age 3

"That was eighty pounds ago, Mom. Let's get vanilla bean freezes." You can't let my mom get started—if she had her way, we'd be frozen in preschool. Luckily, Fern likes being the baby.

I check my ears in the rearview mirror as I get in the backseat. The little gold balls gleam. "I wish I could go show Brooke right now. Or Nora. Or Hui Zong. Or . . . No offense, Mom," since this is our special alone-time together.

"Give your earlobes a chance to go back to their regular color. How are they feeling?"

"Great." Or a hundred times better than I thought they would. Maybe a tinch of throbbing.

tinch

tinch A tiny pinch (my own personal word, which you have my permission to use)

"So what're you up to in gym class these days?" Mom asks.

"Rhythmic gymnastics," I answer.

"Rope climbing was always my least favorite."

"Rope climbing is extinct, Mom."

OTHER EXTINCT THINGS from Mom's day:

gym suits

walking a mile to the bus

phones with cords

"I thought you loved gymnastics, Kate! How many thousands of cartwheels and handstands have I watched, not counting the hundreds I banned?"

PLACES USED to CALL (literally) MY NAME

KATE!

BANK — LOBBY — "Do a hand stand!"

MARKET — AISLE — "Try a cartwheel!"

HOTEL — HALLWAY — "Round off, please!"

FIELD — "WALKOVER, WALKOVER!"

"Zero thousands since third grade. The rhythmic part is dancing."

"And . . . ?"

How does she always know there's more? "We have to dance with boys."

She looks at me in her mirror. "It's just a gym unit, Kate. You'll get through it."

Mom's E.S.P.

STOP HERE

Rocky is the first one to ~~see~~ lick my pierced ears. "Don't let him, Kate!" My mom calls Rocky over.

APPARENTLY it's only a myth DOGS' MOUTHS ARE CLEANER THAN OURS

Fern is second. She immediately asks for pierced ears and gets Mom's famous Geller Family answer.

what MOM says: when you're ten.

what FERN hears: NEVER.

"C'mon, Fern. I have something for you," I say before she can start crying. She follows me up to my desk.

"These?" She picks up my Lego people. I shake my head and open the top drawer. "These?" She points to the box of rubber stamps I keep in the front of the drawer. "These?" She is eyeing my pencil toppers. I wish she'd stop—I was *trying* to be generous.

I hand her a box. "These."

My CLIP-ON, STICK-ON, EVERYTHING-but-PIERCED EARRING COLLECTION

"ALL of them?!" She peels and sticks two earrings on each ear.

"Want some help? How about a mirror?"

OFFERS to HELP FERN	
Accepted	Rejected
IIII'	⊬⊬ ⊬⊬ ⊬⊬ ⊬⊬ ⊬⊬ ⊬⊬ ⊬⊬ ⊬⊬ ⊬⊬ (over)

She gets her jewelry box from under her bed, pops open the lid, and smiles at herself in the little diamond mirror while the ballerina twirls to the music. She adds two fake hoops to each ear, dumps the rest in the bottom of her ballerina box, and says, "Let's go back down!"

"Wow! Somebody got her ears pierced!" My dad puts his hands on my shoulders and studies my ears. "Perfect! And who do we have here, Mrs. Earringalingadingdong?" He scoops Fern up.

Robin smiles. "It's like you've had them forever." It's true, I already can't remember what my ears looked like before.

"Don't you all have something to do? I have to get my ear-themed dinner going." Dad shoos us out of the kitchen.

After we've finished eating, Dad swaps Bob for his plate. "Anybody want to disagree with Bob, or Philip Barry?"

LAST NIGHT'S PICK:
(Another one by Dad)

The time to make up your mind about people is never.
— Philip Barry

"I admit, I made up my mind about you people a long time ago—wacky."

"Wacky apples never fall far from the wacky tree," Mom adds.

"Moving on—let's see if Bob has something ear-related for us. . . ." Dad picks a slip. "Ah, another from our genius-friend Einstein."

Einstein was better at math than my dad's soccer coach.

Two hours later:

"Kate, you awake?" Robin is standing in my doorway. (Usually I go to *her* room.)

I tiptoe over. "Yeah. It kind of hurts to sleep on my ears." The hall light is in my eyes.

"I told Mom and Dad I'd take you with me to Grace's next Tuesday."

"I have a flute lesson—"

"It's Veterans Day. Mom and Dad have to work, and Fern has school. It'll be fun. Grace's sister, Eva, is going to hang out with us; she's in your grade."

"I know. She's in Nora's class, but it's not like we have any of the same friends or—"

"Eva's in the band. She plays the—"

We both say, "Trumpet."

"Did anybody consider asking me? I'd rather go to Brooke's."

druth·er
Your preferences, what you'd rather

'd rather

"Brooke is doing something with her cousins. And Nora's mom has to work. She's taking Nora with her to the mall," Robin says. "Look, if you don't go, I have to stay home and babysit. . . ." She rolls a pair of my sweatpants into a donut.

MY DRUTHERS

1. Go to Brooke's.
2. Go to the mall with Nora.
3. Go back to bed with a book.
4. Alphabetize my bookshelves.
5. Clean Fern's side of the room.

yes, seriously!

"Besides, I really want you to meet Will." She puts the sweatpants on my pillow. "Here, sleep on these. That's what I did the first night."

"Do Eva and I have to run?" (Running is *not* my favorite.)

Robin picks up my K8 ball. "Very doubtful. Unless Eva's rabbit gets loose again. That thing is fast. Sleep tight, Kate!" Her hair brushes my face when she kisses my forehead.

I DREAMED EVA'S RABBIT GOT LOOSE....

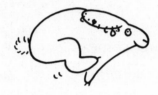

HEAR YE, HEAR YE

"Nice earrings, Kate!" Gene smiles.

"Thanks, Gene!" I smile back. I owe him a ton of compliments.

COMPLIMENTS for GENE?

1. ~~I like your shirt.~~ dumb.
2. ~~I like your haircut.~~ He's bald.
3. ~~You're a great driver.~~ f like I know anything about driving.
4. You're the world's Best Bus driver. USED ✓✓✓ ✓✓

Nora picks up her backpack so I can sit down. "Wow, you really did it! I mean, I knew you would. I couldn't. How bad was it?"

I make a zero. "And you could, if you wanted. I'll go with—" I stop. We both realize it at the same time.

SHE'S MOVING!

"Was the earring gun really loud next to your ear?"

"She used a needle."

"Oh, the needle. Could you hear it piercing the skin?"
I shake my head no. "What did Brooke say when she
saw—?"

"You're the first person to see them, besides my
family."

"And Gene." Nora pulls the strings on her hoodie
tighter. "They look nice."

Brooke makes a big deal about my ears when we get
off the bus. "Wow, they look so good with your hair
behind your ears like that. Makes me want to wear
my gold balls. We can wear matching earrings for
the performance."

"Performance?" Nora turns to Brooke.

"Gymnastics," Brooke says. "Didn't Kate tell you?
Colin's on our team!"

"I'm trying *not* to think about it. Thank you," I say.

Nora smiles and goes to her locker.

When Brooke and I get to homeroom, Mrs. Block invites me to come over to her side of the desk. She looks at my ears. "Very nice, Kate! Maybe I should get mine repierced."

"My doctor could do them," I offer. I don't want Mrs. Block to end up in one of Nora's horror stories.

Note for Mrs. B.'s file
She used = to have pierced ears.

We are all (even Peter Buttrick) behaving perfectly after lunch recess because Mrs. Block is not in the room and she could technically walk in at any minute. Then we hear the clanging.

Oyez, Oyez! Hear ye, hear ye!

"Citizenry of 5B: There will be a meeting held in the Town Hall on the third Thursday of the month of November wherein ye shall decide whether or not to join the forces of Revolution! All will be heard!

Civil discourse shall harness the winds of discord! God save the King!"

God save *me*! Mrs. Block is giving us new identities again. "Citizen Ronan! Citizen Hui Zong! Citizen Kate!" We each get a packet. Mine has "Quaker" written on it. I try to see what's on Hui Zong's, but she's covering it up.

Mrs. B. claps and says, "Let's keep our identities secret. Twenty percent of you are loyal to the King of England. Thirty percent of you are neutral. And the remaining fifty percent are Patriots, also known as the Sons of the Revolution. It should make for a very interesting meeting."

"Yes, very!" Eliza says with her hand still up since she hasn't been called on. "Because thirty percent neutral equals nine of us plus somebody's leg or something. And twenty percent for the king means that three-fifths of one person is loyal, but who knows about the other two-fifths." Eliza is a mega-mathlete.

"That's the problem with apportioning people, isn't it?" Mrs. Block smiles. "Finish reading your packets about the causes and events leading up to the American Revolution by Friday and start to think about your point of view." She gives her bell one last clang and removes her tricornered hat. "Let's line up for library! And band members, let's not forget our instruments."

Brooke and I grab our flutes. We keep our identities secret during library. And band. Then on the way to Junior Guides, Brooke says, "I'll tell you if you tell me . . . Native American!"

"Quaker. Do you think the Quakers were Patriots?"
Brooke shrugs. "Are we
at least on the same
side?" I ask.

"I'm pretty sure Mrs. B.
wrote 'Patriots' for
Patriots," Brooke says.
"We're not Patriots."

MY TURN to be on the
WINNING SIDE of
HISTORY
(or at least on Brooke's side)

LAST TIME
I was Columbus
the ˅Deplored Explorer

GET READY, GET SET

This is Mrs. Staughton's two-month anniversary as Junior Guide leader. She is definitely getting used to the job. For example, when she does the quiet signal now, her underarm sweat stain is half the size of the one she had in September. (Of course the cooler weather also helps.) The snacks are all out.

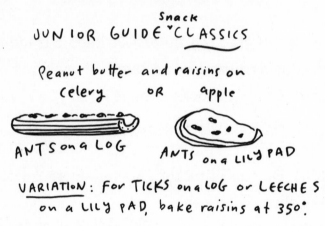

JUNIOR GUIDE Snack CLASSICS

Peanut butter and raisins on
celery   OR   apple

ANTS on a LOG   ANTS on a LILY PAD

VARIATION: For TICKS on a LOG or LEECHES
on a LILY PAD, bake raisins at 350°.

"Allie, shall we get things rolling?" Mrs. S. suggests after everyone has served herself. Allie is Pod President for the month of November. I set my stopwatch and look at Brooke.

"2:16," Brooke mouths.

IT'S TIME to PLAY...
GUESS HOW LONG
~ before ~
MRS. S. TAKES OVER

0:00

"3:39," I whisper back.

After Allie leads the Promise, she announces, "Today we'll get started on the Harvest Food Drive contest. Everything's the same as last year, except this year we're going to beat the boys!" She raises her fist toward the ceiling and almost takes Mrs. S.'s chin with it. "Pod 429 will get the overnight at Luau Keys. Pack 22—"

"Pardon, let me step in here for just a second, Allie," Mrs. S. says.

NO WINNER !
(you must
guess within
ten seconds.)

"4:21, new record!" I whisper to Brooke.

"I don't know who came up with this idea of a *contest*—but I strongly oppose it. It runs counter to the principles of service: community, compassion. A contest is just plain . . ."

↖ SUGGESTION: Fun!

Mrs. S. doesn't finish that thought. "Let's leave competition on the soccer field. I'm going to speak with Pack 22's leader. I'd like to collaborate—that's a fifty-cent word for work together—then I'm sure we can find a way we could all celebrate."

"Back to you, Allie," Mrs. S. says.

"That's okay, I'm done." Allie sits down.

"Now, I don't know how you've done your collecting in years past . . . ," Mrs. S. says, and pulls the easel with the pad of paper closer.

"Mrs. Lawrence gave us a script," Lily says.

"I see, well, during our craft time today, we are going to 'craft' our own scripts. I made two different graphic organizers!" She snaps the cap back on her marker when she's finished explaining the second one and says, "So let's pick partners and pen pitches." (*Translation:* Her fifty-cent word for script.)

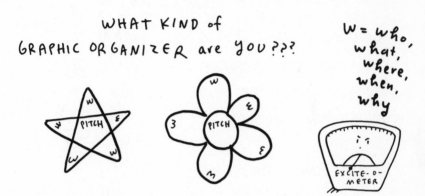

WHAT KIND of GRAPHIC ORGANIZER are YOU???

PITCH

PITCH

W = who, what, where, when, why

EXCITE-O-METER

As secretary for our threesome, I aim my pencil at Brooke. "First W: who?"

"Me?" Brooke says. "You mean like, 'My name is Brooke or Guide's name . . .'" That's how Mrs. Lawrence's script always started.

My name is _____.
                   GUIDE'S NAME

"Don't your friends and neighbors already know who you are?" Nora says.

"Okay, let's skip who. What?" I look at Nora.

"What? I hate Luau Keys. Once when my sister went, there was a piece of poop on the bottom of the pool. They said it was a Tootsie Roll, but Tootsie Rolls float. So I hope we don't win."

"Then maybe you should quit," Heather Staughton barges in. "My mother said you're moving anyway."

HEATHER is
MRS. S.'s daughter.

"Heather," Nora says with this big weird smile, "that is the *best* idea you've ever had. I quit." Mrs. Staughton is busy packing up the ants-on-the-log-stumps and misses the whole thing.

"Wait, don't quit," I say. "I was really looking forward to doing the neighborhood together."

"Kate's right," Brooke agrees. "At least wait until her mom gets here, because if you're serious about quitting, you want to be able to make a quick exit."

At 4:51, Allie blows a harmonica and hands it back to Mrs. Staughton, who is shaking her head and muttering to her fanny pack, "Where have you hidden my pitch pipe?"

"Let's circle up and read our scripts," Allie says.

When it's our turn, Nora, who is no longer showing any signs of quitting, reads ours.

Hello, my name is (you know). I am with Junior Guide Pod (you know). I would like to ask for your help with (what everyone else already said). Thank you, them, for saying it so I didn't have to.

Mrs. Staughton takes over one last time. "Before we leave, let's close our eyes and imagine a successful Harvest Food Drive." She is the only one with her eyes closed when she says, "Now, open! Let us each share one successful Harvest Food Drive word in closing. I'll begin. Abundance!"

"Squish in," my mom says when we get to the car. Fern's in the backseat. "Dad's stuck in a meeting. How was Junior Guides?"

Nora is inspecting her side for Fern-food before it ends up on her pants, so I answer, "Does that mean no tacos tonight?" (Tacos are definitely Top 5.)

"You think Dad is the only one who can make tacos?" My mom shakes her head. "So what's the plan for the Harvest Food Drive?"

"The plan *was* to beat Pack 22"—present company ← AKA Nora
not included—"but Mrs. Staughton wants us to col-lab-o-rate instead. Nora and I are doing Pugh Road together." Present company is now thumb-wrestling with Fern and does not object.

"Sounds good!" My mom turns into Nora's driveway. I open my door to let her out. She's still wrestling. "I think we better call the match a tie," my mom says.

If you QUIT and no one HEARS you...

"No way, I won!" Fern squeals. "I beat a— How old are you, Nora?" Nora wiggles all ten fingers.

"Stop moving, I can't count them!"

"Thanks for letting her win," I say to Nora once she is out of the car.

"I'm the world's worst quitter," she says. "I'll get off the bus at your house tomorrow."

imPERFECT PITCH

"Have fun!" Gene calls after us as we run up my driveway. I was going to call back, "It's work, Gene. Harvest Food Drive!" But then I remembered I promised Nora it would be fun.

"Fun, according to the girl who *likes* talking to strangers . . . ," Nora says.

"Strangers, according to the girl who doesn't talk to her neighbors," I reply.

"Good point. I'll remember that for my *next* neighborhood."

Rocky greets Nora like it's been four years (not four days) since he last saw her. My dad holds on to her backpack so she can step out of it. "Welcome, Nora 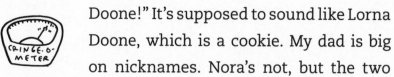 Doone!" It's supposed to sound like Lorna Doone, which is a cookie. My dad is big on nicknames. Nora's not, but the two of them bonded last month planning the haunted house for my tenth birthday party.

"Can I make you some popcorn?" my dad offers. Nora watches him while Rocky and I collect copies of our pitch, my stapler, and all the paper supermarket bags I can find.

THINGS NORA LOVES
1. Hoodies 🍀
2. Popcorn //
3. Haunted houses
4. me (just kidding)

"Don't let me rush you," my dad says, tipping us off our stools. "But it gets dark early now."

We start at the Bellinos next door. Nora nudges me. "You go first!"

Fritzy is barking his little head off down around Mrs. Bellino's knees. I hold up the empty supermarket bag, and Mrs. Bellino nods, mouthing, "I'll fill it and bring it over." She makes finger-steps across her palm.

Nora rings the bell at the next place. "Your turn again. Fritzy's doesn't count."

Mr. Hughes asks, "Who's your friend, Kate?"

"This is Nora Klein. Nora, Mr. Hughes."

"And what brings you to my door, Nora?"

I hand her the pitch.

Hello, my name is ·Skip THAT· I am with
Junior Pod Guide ∹ Junior God Puide &
I am with Kate and we would like to
ask for your help to help us help others
OH HELP! I would like to turn into
a NONPERISHABLE FOOD ITEM.

"It's Nora's first year," I explain. "We're doing the
Harvest Food Drive. If you want to help, we can leave
a bag and pick it up Sunday."

"I'll take two of your bags, please."

Nora hands them over and says, "Thank you."

"Thank YOU, Nora. You girls are doing all the hard
work." Mr. Hughes steps back inside.

"That's it, I am pitching these papers!" Nora stomps
ahead.

"Don't! We'll need them if no one is home." I take the pitches.

Nora does fine with Mrs. Rogers. "Wait there—let me take care of this right now." She returns with a bulging bag and holds it out to Nora.

"Uh, Mrs. Rogers, we still have a few more houses— is it okay if we come back for your bag on Sunday?" I ask while Nora is rounding up the last can.

Mrs. Rogers slides everything into a new plastic bag. "Sunday is fine. I'll leave your cans on this green chair, if I decide to go out."

"Wow, this is *some* fun, Kate!" Nora shouts as she cuts across the next yard.

"Hold on, not that one." There's a light on over the door, but the rest of the house is dark.

"Oh, c'mon, you know I *love* a haunted house!"

"It's not haunted, just a little spooky. Mrs. Verlangen takes forever to get to the door, and we're not supposed to bother her anyway. She's on a fixed income. And not the next house, either. That's Josh Wieden's." Josh is in Pack 22.

Nobody's home at the house next to Josh's, so we staple the pitch onto a shopping bag and lean it against the front door. "They'll really fill it?"

skep·ti·cal
Doubtful

Yeah? No, I don't think so.

"They did two years ago. Last year, Josh did the whole neighborhood before the pod had our first food drive meeting."

"Oh." Nora takes her hands out of her sweatshirt pockets. "Want some?"

"That belongs to Mrs. Rogers!!!"

"No, she gave it to us." Nora is lifting the pull tab.

"Nora, she gave it to the food drive." I wait for the *pffft* of the lid.

"Fine, if that's the way you feel about it," Nora says, and puts it back in her pocket. We stop at four more houses, then call it a night.

Mrs. Klein is talking to my dad when we walk in. Nora runs upstairs to my room.

"Is Pod 429 going to Luau Keys?" She chants, "Please no, please no" as she turns my K8 ball over: "Better not tell you now."

"See?" Nora says. "It doesn't want you to be disappointed!" She turns it over again. "Don't count on it."

"It's telling *you* not to count on *me* being the disappointed one," I argue. Her mother is calling her. "Here." I hold out my hand. "You're addicted to that thing."

She turns it over one last time.

TGIFFF

The next morning, Dad slides over so I can put my bowl in the sink. "I have a homework question," I say.

He looks the way you should look when someone tells you there is NO homework. "Were Quakers for or against the American Revolution?"

YOU KNOW YOU'RE GROWN UP WHEN...

I LOVE homework questions!

"Go-o-o-o-o-d question."

My personal observation: Go-o-o-o-o-d questions have lo-o-o-o-ong answers. "Okay, but the bus'll be here in three minutes."

"Tell me what you know so far."

"They came to America for religious freedom, so I know they aren't on the king's side. But they're pacifists."

"It's complicated. They each had to make up their own minds, much like I suspect Mrs. Block is expecting

57

you to. Grammalolo is a Quaker. Why don't you ask her? And THE-E-E-ERE's your bus . . . ," he says, opening the door so I can sprint out.

NOW I KNOW TWO QUAKERS:
QUAKER OATS·MAN   GRAMMALOLO

When we walk into school, Allie waves Nora, Brooke, and me over. Heather is holding a box. "Guess what!" Allie says.

Nora guesses, "It's Bring Your Pod President to School Day!"

Brooke and I laugh. Allie goes on, "Very funny. Heather wrote an announcement, and Mr. Lovejoy says he'll read it!"

MR. L's P.U. AWARD-WINNING READING

The school store will be open from 8 until — er, the school store is now closed. It's time for the fourth annual Farley Fall Food Drive. CAN #1: Can I help? CAN #2: Yes, you can-- CORRECTION: MAY I help? Yes, you may. Place your food items in the specially marked bins. And let's make this another super-fine Farley Friday!

"Lovejoy kills the announcement," Brooke mumbles.

"And Block kills 'free writing.'" Mrs. Block winks at Brooke. "This morning I'd like you to write as your Town Meeting characters. You've read your research packets." Mrs. Block is nodding like a bobblehead. "Now you're going to begin to breathe some life into this material. . . ."

At least she's admitting the research packet material is dead! I stare at my journal until the blue lines wobble.

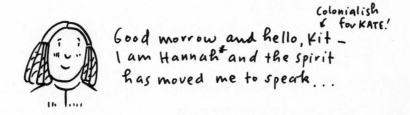

Colonialish & for KATE!

Good morrow and hello, Kit — I am Hannah* and the spirit has moved me to speak . . .

"We came to America to practice our religion." *Check, know that.* "I do not have oatmeal for breakfast." *Seriously?* "I eat porridge. When I am sewing, my heart is calm." Hannah disappears, and I know naught (colonialish for zero) about sewing, but I am moved to make up the rest of her day.

*I LOVE palindromes!

We have to act like our Town Meeting characters in social studies at the end of the day. You can tell Hui Zong and Eliza are both Patriots by the questions they ask: "Why did *we* have to pay for that King's war?"

They are talking about the French and Indian War in 1754, which I thought was the French and Native Americans against the British, but apparently Native Americans fought for both sides because Brooke seems to be siding with the king of England.

The KING

George III
aka
George William Frederick
1738 - 1820 ↑
last
name

"I am not *for* the Revolution," I tell Brooke as we are packing up. "But I am against the king. He punished Quakers for not belonging to the Church of England. And, personally, if he didn't need you to beat the French, I don't think the king would have lifted a royal finger to help Native Americans. Don't you want to be neutral together?" Brooke doesn't say anything, so I change the subject. "What're you doing tomorrow?"

"Delivering my food drive bags."

"Oh, Nora and I did that yest—"

"I know."

"We're collecting on Sunday. Want to come?"

"That's okay. It's your thing with Nora."

"My thing? With Nora?" The bell rings. Oh, so this is not about the Native Americans and Quakers. "Wait—Brooke, it's the *pod's* thing." She

My THINGS:
1. Drawing (not super. realistic)
2. Sleepovers
3. Reading
4. Jokes (especially with BFF)
5. Cooking
6. Sports

doesn't say a word the whole way down the hall. "Is Sunday a maybe?" I ask right before she heads to her bus.

"Call me." At least that's something.

WEAK-END

"Mom, I'm already bored and the weekend hasn't even started. Everyone's busy." I drop my backpack and Rocky comes running.

ROCKY IS NEVER BORED.

"How 'bout 'Hi, Mom, how was *your* day?'" She gives me a hug. "I'm working tomorrow morning, but I could do something with you in the afternoon."

"I meant doing something with a kid, no offense."

"Well, you could give Fern a little time. What about practicing basketball?"

"By myself? None of my friends play."

from mom's SUGGESTION BOX

Give Rocky a bath!

Practice your flute!

Clean your room!

write thank-you notes!

whee! SUPER-FUN!

"Robin mentioned that Grace's sister is trying out, the one she's giving her horses—"

~ NOT her FUTURE HUSBAND'S FAMILY

"She's giving her horses to Eva?!"

EVA
The Ideal Big Little Sister

"Kate, you have never shown an interest in a single one of those horses."

"What about Fern? The collection should stay in the family, *our* family."

FLASH-BACK! "It's your THING with NORA."

"Is something else bothering you, Monkey?"

"I think I'll go for a bike ride," I answer.

MOMCO REMIND·O·MATIC

"Put something warm on."

Go to the bathroom
Wash your hands
Don't forget your manners
Be careful
Be home before dark

"I'm—"

"Ten, yes, I know. Your father is forty-one and I still remind him. I'm a mother." She pulls my hood strings tight. "And a lawyer. Now quit arguing with me."

The cold air makes my eyes water, but it clears my head: Brooke and I have been best friends since third grade. We just had a bad ~~day~~ 5 DAYS. We'll always be best friends. Not that I really want Nora to move, but everything will go back to the way it was after she does. Won't it?

 On Saturday morning, I take my mother's suggestion—I try to play with Fern, but her play date keeps playing with me and now Fern is crying. "Champ," my dad steps in. "I mean this in the nicest way: why don't you go to your room for a while?"

"A while" = the rest of the day, except lunch. I practice my flute. Read my book. And I spend 2½ hours working on new duct tape items.

I am arranging my new samples before Grammalolo (aka my best customer/worst critic) arrives. "Wow, looks like you had a very proDUCTive afternoon," my dad says.

FROM MY FAMOUS DUCT TAPE

KATE·A·LOG

flower barrette

100% leak·proof cup

ONE-SIZE* bracelet *yours!

LARGE phonecase

especially for Brooke's glasses case

backpack I.D. (or Nora's flute case)
Name...... School.....Rm... Phone......

·burp- catcher (just kidding!)

"None of these really suit me," Grammalolo says without giving me a chance to make my presentation. "Can I hire you to design a checkbook holder, special order? I know—the rest of the world is using the Internet and credit cards—Now, there's an idea for you! Have you done a credit card holder?" She hands me a ten-dollar bill. "What are you saving for these days?"

Um. My wish list is actually pretty empty since I just had my birthday last month. "My education." Or hockey skates, which are educational for my feet.

"*Speaking of education, Lois*"—this is Dad's CPR for dying conversation—"Kate is studying the Quakers in social studies."

This could have been a nice conversation...

Do you know whether Quakers were FOR or AGAINST the Revolution?

which?

EGYPT?

American.

I'm not THAT old, dear!

Mom says, "I didn't hear you come in." She kisses Grammalolo on the cheek. Her so-called "morning of work" took the entire day.

"I was just making a purchase from Snickelfritz here," Grammalolo says.

"And did Snickelfritz show you her ears?" my mom asks. I forget the whole world*hasn't seen them by now.

*Except the SENTINELESE

Grammalolo's face softens. "I'll be able to wear your birthday earrings in eight—seven weeks and three days," I tell her.

"I hope they bring you as much pleasure as they

and others who cannot OR do not wish to be contacted by the outside world.

brought me." She lifts my chin. "Tell me a little more about this social studies project of yours."

"Why don't you two go sit in the living room and I'll bring you some drinks," my dad says.

I tell Grammalolo about Hannah and the Town Meeting. "Quakers have often been on the side of change or revolution. Independence and freedom are Quaker ideals," Grammalolo explains. "You, er, Hannah can join the forces for revolution without using force—you'll need to find peaceful ways of 'fighting' for your beliefs. I believe the Quakers led some of the boycotts—see what you can find out about that." I make a note on my napkin. "There are two 't's in boycott—I suppose you would have figured that out. Keep me posted. Of course, I know how it turns out. . . ."

BUFFET of MIRACLES

GRAMMALOLO DOESN'T CRITICIZE my MANNERS

MASHED POTATOES AND GRAVY

APPLE PIE à la MODE

FULL MOON 9 x 5:23 p.m.

GRAMMA LOLO GIVES ME HER MODE

MONKEY (me) in the MIDDLE

Mrs. Klein drops Nora and Brooke off on Sunday afternoon. "I didn't know you were coming!!!" I say.

Reasons why Brooke
is my best friend:

#14. I can always
count on her.

"Yeah, well." Brooke shrugs.

My dad shakes his keys. "Anybody need any extra fortification—snack, drink, hair elastic, hand sanitizer, chewing gum, pit stop, sweatshirt, dental floss?" He gets two no's and a "Dental floss, Dad?!" "Then away we go!" He smiles and unlocks the car doors.

Brooke and I slide in, while Nora brushes off her side of the seat and sits down. "Good afternoon. I will be your collection driver. Please let me know if there is anything I can do to make your ride more—"

The DAD Control

"Can you put on Kiss 108 please, Mr. Geller?" Brooke asks.

He flips the radio on. "First stop?"

"Bellinos'," I answer.

My dad turns the car around while we run up the Bellinos' walk. Fritzy is barking and throwing himself against the door, but there's no sign of Mrs. Bellino. Brooke rings the bell, and the house goes completely silent. Nora's eyes get big.

Five seconds later Fritzy is barking again.

"Not home!" I yell to my dad. He's waiting by the car.

"Is your sister on Fritzy duty? Mrs. Bellino probably gave her the bag. Where next?"

"Hugheses'. We'll walk, Dad." Brooke and I run.

"Wait!" Nora yells like the word has two syllables, and she walks even more slowly while Brooke and I are *way-eighting*.

Mr. Hughes opens the door and steps partway out. "Hello, Nora and Kate, and I don't believe we've met."

"Brooke Johnson."

"I'm sorry, Brooke Johnson, I don't have a bag for you."

"Two bags is awesome!" Nora steps in front of Brooke and takes one bag, then hands me the other one. "Brooke is just helping us . . . to help you . . . to help others . . . ? Thank you, Mr. Hughes!"

"It doesn't really matter whose bag is which," Brooke says as we're heading back to the car. "They all go the same place."

"It's her first year," I remind Brooke. Plus different things matter to different people, and Nora, as we know, is different.

There are no cars in the Rogerses' garage. "She said she'd leave the bag on the green chair by the door!" Nora yells to Brooke, who is already on the porch.

"Looks like she left *your* bag on that bench," my dad says, pointing.

"You can carry it." Brooke hands the bag to Nora and takes off running.

Nora hands me the bag and runs after Brooke even though Nora knows it's Mrs. Verlangen's house.

"STOP!" I yell. Neither one of them is listening, so I have to sprint to catch up.

"This place is creepy." Brooke is standing a few feet from the door.

"We're not supposed to be here," I say, glaring at Nora. **ver·bo·ten**
Forbidden

"Kate says it's not haunted, but you can tell she's afraid to go near it." Nora laughs. Brooke starts to laugh, then covers her mouth.

"You two can do whatever you want. Leave me out of it." *Oh, never mind, you already did.*

TAXI!

You can pick Nora & Brooke up now!

"Oh, c'mon, Kate, we're almost done. Your neighbors don't know me," Brooke says.

"Me either," Nora says. The two of them hang back while I do the last four houses.

Nora's mom and mine are working on the crossword puzzle at the kitchen table when we get home.

"Mom, you're early!" Nora says.

From the same page of the

"Nice to see you, too," Mrs. Klein says, and the grown-ups laugh. "We're meeting Granny and Poppop at Swifty's for an early supper."

MOTHER-DAUGHTER JOKE BOOK

"Just a sec, I have to get something I left in Kate's room." Nora runs upstairs. Weird, considering we haven't been in my room all day. I look at Brooke, but she doesn't look up from the puzzle.

Two minutes later, Nora plants her can of SpaghettiOs in the center of the kitchen table. "I almost forgot this one!"

"What was that doing in your room?" Brooke asks.

It's a good question, but I don't have a chance to answer. Mrs. Klein hands Nora the can and says, "Put it in the car with the rest. I told the Gellers I'd drop your haul off at school next week."

"One last thing!" Nora runs upstairs again. If she takes any longer than forty-five seconds, I am going to go up after her. She comes down with her hood up and her hands stuffed into her sweatshirt pockets. "I don't believe in your K8 ball."

Brooke and I race up to my room as soon as Nora's gone. "What do you think she asked? I'll lift it,"

Brooke says. "Reallllly carefully ... what does it say?"

"Hold on, I need my flashlight." I lie on my back and shine it on my K8 ball.

We look at each other. "I have no idea—last time she asked about the food drive. This seemed—she seemed pretty upset."

"She totally believes in it," Brooke says. She sloshes the ball around and turns it over. "Do you?"

"Me? It's just fun," I say. I shine the flashlight on her. "You?"

"Same. Quit pointing that at me!" I turn the flashlight off. "What are you doing Tuesday?"

"My parents are working, so I have to go to the Paysons' with Robin."

"Ooh, fun, race training! I know how you love running."

"Eva and I are going to practice for basketball tryouts. I don't mind running if—no offense to soccer—you can score more than one point an hour."

Brooke stops pulling the spiral notebook fringes off my Books I've Read list and looks at me like I did something wrong. "What?" I ask.

Brooke shakes her head. "Never mind."

"Your cousins are around, right?"

"Cousins? They're not coming. My mom signed me up for something. She's working, too." Brooke gets busy with the paper fringes again. Headlights make shadows on my bunk curtain. "That's her, gotta go." Brooke runs downstairs, hardly saying goodbye.

GO BACK to NORMAL

I follow her. "Hey, wait!" If I knew what was wrong, I could possibly fix it. I yell from the garage as she's opening the car door. "Want to do something tomorrow?"

"I have an eye doctor's appointment." She sits down, then bobs back up. "Thank you, and thank your parents for me." Her mom made her say that.

One second, I'm sitting on the garage steps leaning against the kitchen door. Next, I'm lying on the kitchen floor, looking up at my mom. "Sorry, Kate, I didn't know you were on the other side of the door. . . ."

"Next year, the food drive can be Brooke and Nora's thing—they can go to any house they want."

"Rough day?" Mom gives me a hand up. "Next year, Nora won't be here. And I thought this was everybody's last year of Junior Guides."

"So much for it being the best year."

Sometimes I swear Bob is psychic. Or Dad goes through the papers and picks one out ahead of time (aka cheats).

> The most I can do for my friend is be his friend.
> —Henry David Thoreau

← Right part (considered "radical" for men.)

Henry David Thoreau
American Author
1817-1862

I call Brooke after I'm finished clearing the table. Mrs. Johnson answers. "Brooke is practicing her flute, Kate. Can it wait until tomorrow?" She's never made me wait.

"I had this idea . . . that I could go with Brooke to the eye doctor's and help her pick out new glasses . . . if she wants," I say.

"It's a nice idea, Kate. The eye doctor only prescribes the glasses. Besides, I can't remember the last time Brooke got new frames. . . ."

What if my friend won't let me be her friend?

78

VETERANS DAY, EVE, and EVA

"So, what are you going to do at the mall all day tomorrow?" I'm just making conversation with Nora on the bus ride home. I actually know the answer because I've been to the mall with her twice, which is the most times I've been to the mall with anybody besides my mother.

"My mom has a plan." She is retying the knots on her sweatshirt strings.

"My mom made a plan for me, too. I'm going to the Paysons'."

"Eva Payson's in my class. She's tolerable."

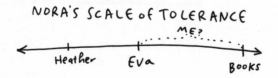

NORA'S SCALE OF TOLERANCE

Heather — Eva — ME? — BOOKS

I stand up so she can get out at her stop. "See you Wednesday!" I say.

"Is buhbye ubbi dubbi for bye?" Nora asks. I'm still thinking when she comes out with, "Toodles!"

Two boys in the back yell "Toodles" out the window. Nora's head drops and she keeps walking. I'm surprised Gene doesn't do anything. Then one of them gets off the bus and Gene says, "You can say toodles to your bus privileges next time you pull something like that." He opens the doors for the toodler and looks back to make sure everyone got his point.

GENE SCORES!

~~HHt~~ thousand
H.D. Thoreau
points

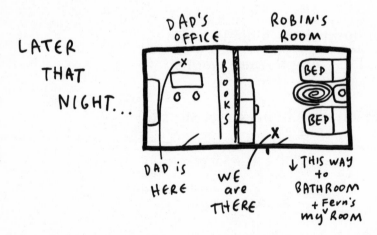

LATER THAT NIGHT...

DAD'S OFFICE

ROBIN'S ROOM

BOOKS

BED

BED

DAD is HERE

WE are THERE

↓ THIS WAY to BATHROOM + Fern's my ⌄ ROOM

"What're you doing?" Robin whispers. "Dad's still in his office!"

"I can't sleep," I say. "I really wish I was going to Brooke's. Her cousins aren't coming and stuff is weird between us—we could have had the whole day to fix it. No offense, I mean, I want to meet Will, but that'll only take five minutes and then I have to spend the rest of the day with a stranger, Eva."

"We'll all do stuff together. Maybe we can go to the movies—"

"Isn't that kind of like a date?"

The Egg Thing

"Going to the movies alone is a date, Kate. Maybe you and Brooke need to take a little break from each other. Come here." I sit on the edge of her other bed. "I'll do the egg thing." After three imaginary eggs, I'm feeling very sleepy.

♫ ♫ ♪

"Tuesday, Tuesday!" I put my pillow over my head. Nothing against the Beatles, everything against my dad—the singing alarm clock. "Rise and shine, Mrs. Slug-a-Bed!"

"Wake me up when Fern gets out of the bathroom, please!" I say into my pillow.

My dad flicks on the light. "Fern and your mother are long gone. I want to see two feet, yours, on the floor!"

"Okay, okay, okay, okay." I okay all the way to the bathroom and shut the door. I consider falling back asleep on the toilet, just to see if it's even possible, and then Robin knocks.

I'M an EXCELLENT SLEEPER

Age 4

Slept
through
fireworks

Age 7

Slept through
dinner
(I was sick.)

Age 9

Slept through
second half of
Fern's recital

"Last one to the table has to eat the rest of Dad's special eggs!" she says as she bounces down the stairs.

"Okay, I will, W-I-L-L." I make kiss noises just to bug her. Besides, if she really wanted to go to Grace's, we'd get there faster if she ate all the eggs.

"Sorry, Champ, you snooze, you lose!" My dad holds up the empty egg pan. "Have a peanut butter and Nutella on toast. Your sister's waiting in the car."

SCORE!

Robin, Grace, Eva, and I are standing around the Paysons' kitchen table, staring at a plate of mini muffins. "Eva made them," Grace says.

"Oh, cool." (Brooke and I have an annoying habit of saying "cool" when we feel awkward. I forget who started it.) "Do you like to bake?"

Eva nods, and I take one. Blueberry. Not my favorite. I don't like things that pop after they're cooked. "Cool."

I'm counting...

83

"Want to go up to my room?" She doesn't give me any other options, so I follow her. "We have to be quiet—my brother is still sleeping," she whispers.

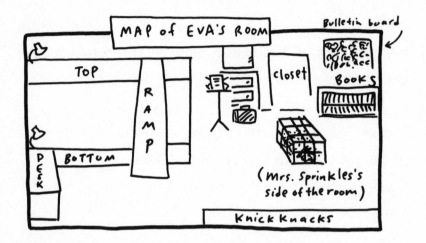

Eva's room is practically an exact copy of mine. Her bunk beds *and* music stand are in the same exact place. She also shares her room. With her rabbit, Mrs. Sprinkles. The cool—ack!—the best part is the ramp up to her top bunk. Eva's dad built it so her dog Molly (who is a boy!) can sleep with her on the top bunk.

She's sitting at the top of the ramp. "Which do you think will roll faster?" She's holding a Silly Putty egg and a bottle of lotion.

"Is there something in the egg?" She lets them both go.

"Correct—egg! Apple or Molly's ball?" Ball wins. Eva takes a bite of the apple. "Now, the roll-off— egg versus ball!" Her dog comes bounding up and grabs the ball just as the roll-off hits the ramp. "Interference! Mol-ly, come back here!"

"We're going running!" Grace yells up.

Eva looks at me. "Want to go?"

Possible answers:

A) Are you #crazy?

B) I'd rather give Mrs. Petty a pedicure. *aka* *PETTYCURE*

C) Is it almost time to go home?

D) Not today.

"Phew," Eva says. "I hate running!"

"Wake Will up if you need anything!" Grace goes on.

"I'm up, I'm up . . . ," Will groans from his bedroom.

"He's up, but believe me, you don't want to see him until he's downstairs. C'mon, let's play basketball."

Eva and I take turns making up our own basketball practice. We're both dribbling with our left hands when she says, "My brother has a crush on your sister. He made me promise not to tell Grace because he knew she'd tell Robin. Swear you won't tell." She holds up her pinky.

"But he didn't make you promise not to tell *me*. . . ." I pinky-swear anyway.

"I'm hungry. Let's go inside. Will!" she yells as she's walking in the kitchen. "We're hungry!"

Will sneaks up behind her and says, "RIGHT HERE!"

(loudly and directly into her ear). She shrieks. He turns to me and says, "You must be the Katester." He holds out his hand, and I shake it.

Will looks a lot like Eva—same shiny, almost-black brown hair and eyes—but he doesn't have her freckles. And you can't see his eyebrows. They're hidden under the hair that swoops across his forehead. "You telling me a couple of ten-year-olds can't make their own snacks?"

"Fine, but then will you help us with our shots?"

"Meet me outside when you're ready." I watch Will shooting in the driveway while Eva gets us Cheerios and chocolate milk.

"Does he ever miss?"

"The other teams usually put two people on him to stop him from shooting."

"All right, Kate." Will passes me the ball. "Show me your best shot!" He watches the ball bounce off the rim and gives it back to me. "Not bad. Now I want you to wave goodbye. Keep that right hand up there. I know what you're thinking—

Hello, I look stupid.

but nobody cares how you look, not when you keep putting them in . . . like that! Nice!"

Grace and Robin get back from their run. "Lunch at Common Grounds, Will?" Grace says.

"It's my day off. How 'bout lunch at the mall?"

"I LOVE shopping!" Eva practically sings.

"I don't!" The words came out before I could stop them.

Will laughs. "Just lunch, no shopping."

HOMONYMOUS: MAUL-MALL

It's 12:59 and I'm starving by the time my sister finishes taking her shower. Will* drives us to the mall. The three of them are going to the Route 66 Diner. "Meet back here, bottom of these escalators, in an hour—sixty minutes. You two got it?"

*AND doing her hair AND make-up AND getting dressed UP

I set my watch-alarm. Eva says, "Yes, sir," and salutes her brother. "C'mon, food court!" We jump on the escalator.

"Did you know that Nora Klein's mom works at this mall?" I say while we look over the first floor. "At Rachel's, Nora gets free cookies, warm, from the oven, and everybody knows her around here." Eva's eyes get wide.

"There she is, that's her, isn't it? That's Nora Klein!" Eva's pointing to Trattoria Joe's at the far end of the food court.

"Nora doesn't like pizz—" Then I see Brooke next to her.

"Let's go say hi," Eva says. NEWS FLASH: I can't move! I have been turned into a piece of petrified wood. She yanks my sleeve. "C'mon—I thought you and Brooke were best friends."

Are we? K8 *Zzz*

Petrified-wood me walks over. (Other me—the one I wish was real—is running 199,000 miles per hour in the opposite direction.) Nora nudges Brooke. Historic frowning first: Brooke sees me and her face falls. P.W.M. keeps walking.

500 Pounds

(O.M. flattened by FACE-falling weight)

Apparently Eva is the only one who knows what to say. "Hi, Nora. Hi, Brooke."

Brooke does this awkward wave, and Nora says, "What are you doing here?"

I can answer that. "Getting lunch. What are *you* doing here?" I look directly at Brooke.

ON a SCALE of AWKWARDNESS

Breathing ←———————×———————→ Forgetting to wear pants to school

WE ARE HERE!

Brooke looks at Nora, so Nora answers, "My mom needed duets for her VIP shoppers again. You and me—well, it was Brooke's turn. I mean, it didn't go so—" Nora stutters. "Do you want them to put extra olives on your pizza?" The pizza line is piling up behind us.

FLASH-BACK!

AHHH!

It's YOU AND I, not me. "I am not exactly hungry right now." Silence. "One of you could have told me." Brooke looks away.

"Whoa, is it one-thirty?" Nora points to my watch. Brooke has said a total of zero words. "We have to get back."

Eva moves so they can pass by. "Sorry," Eva says to me.

"Not your fault," I say.

FOR EXAMPLE -
what if she
eats her slice
in a SICKENING
way?

mLOOK.
MO
HAMS!

"I'm still hungry. Will it make you sick if I eat?" she asks.

Brooke has trained me not to say no automatically. "If you tell them you're Nora's friend, they will give you extra everything, whatever you want."

"No thanks," Eva says, and orders a plain slice and a root beer. "Ginger ale?"

"I'll be fine."

Will, Grace, and Robin are waiting for us at the meeting spot. Robin is staring at me.

"What? We're not late," I say. "My alarm hasn't even gone off yet."

Don't be so OFFensive.

Remember, Kate-peace means to be in the middle of things and still be calm in your heart.

"Kate, no one said you were late," Robin says. "Don't be so defensive."

When we get back to the Paysons', Eva wants to make fingerprint pets. It's hard to concentrate. "Wow, you're a good drawer," she says. Everybody else is used to my drawing. The compliment actually makes me feel a few degrees better.

(SELF PORTRAIT) Drawer

Thanks.

"Let's do something else," Eva says when she finishes her third pet. "Want to spy?" We slip off the top bunk and down the stairs. She opens the basement door. "Are you guys down there?" She makes the "shhh!" signal, and we sneak onto the top step.

"Yeah," the three of them answer.

"Okay, just checking!" she yells, and shuts the door loudly. Eva sneaks down three more stairs and I crouch behind her. She smiles and gives me a thumbs-up. The three of them are watching a movie.

"I can't see," I whisper, so she moves down another stair. Now I can see—Robin and Will are holding hands on the couch. They look like they are about to—ew!—K-I-S-S! EW! I have to turn away.

"What was *that*?!" Will jumps up.

Eva is clutching me, frozen. *If I were a ladybug, my knees would be gushing right now.*

"Sorry? I was just going to show Kate where I am—where I plan to put Robin's horses, and—" Eva stammers.

"It's kind of hard to see—you might want to turn the light on." Will holds up a paintbrush and a crushed,

I mean dented can of mahogany stain. "You weren't planning to stain—I mean spy on us, were you?"

"Saved by the ride!" Robin says. Mom's wheels just went by the window. "Kate, do you have all your stuff?"

Eva comes with me while I get it. "I probably should have warned you," she says. "I'm a terrible spy." We both laugh.

"Kate, hurry, Mom's waiting!" I take the stairs two at a time. "What do you say to Eva?"

what I think:

I say, "my moTHER is out in the car— wHO are you?"

what I say:

Thanks, Eva! I had a really coo-good time.

"Everybody have a good day?" Mom asks once we're moving.

"Eva likes to bake, she doesn't like to run, and we're both bad spies," I answer.

"What were you spying on?" Robin lowers the visor with the mirror so she can see me.

"Do they have a brother?" Mom's looking at me in the rearview mirror.

"Brother? I . . . no."

"Yes!" Robin says. "Will is their brother. Kate?"

"I know, I was saying, 'I know. They do. Have a brother. Will.' Very nice. For a brother. Not that I have one to compare him with, obviously." *HELP?!* "Mom, can we build a ramp to my top bunk so Rocky can sleep up there with me?"

"Maybe . . . after the holidays," Mom says, like I'm perfectly normal. "Your dad's going to pick up some pizza for dinner and—Wow, I didn't expect the stink eye, Kate."

"Oh, no . . . just that I had pizza for lunch."

"Weren't you the girl who told me she could have pizza every meal, every day, every year, and twice on Sunday, for the rest of her life?"

"When I was four. Never mind, Mom, pizza's fine."

I give Rocky his dinner when we get home, then go up to my bottom bunk.

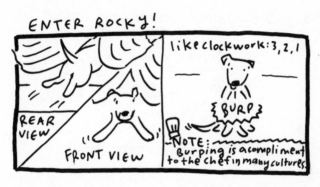

Rocky is making airplane ears at me, like he's waiting for me to say something. "I was so worried Brooke was feeling left out with this food drive collection—and the whole time, she and Nora were leaving *me* out." Rocky lies down and puts his head on my chest. "I don't care. The two of them can be friends, and I'll be friends with Eva."

"Whatcha doin' in there?" Dad knocks on my door. Rocky bolts.

"Is it dinnertime?" I poke my head out between the curtains.

"I'm going to pick up the pizza now. I was snoozing— stayed up too late writing that article last night. Mom says you made a new friend today."

THIS SUMS UP MY DAY :

1 NEW FRIEND **- 2** OLD FRIENDS **=** ☐

"I saw Brooke. With Nora. At the mall."

"I take it that was bad? Your mom didn't mention it."

"They were doing the duets in the VIP lounge—"

"As I recall, your VIP duet experience is *not* one you would care to repeat."

"You don't get it. Both of them knew, and neither one of them told me. I was completely left out. AND lied to."

"That's no good." That makes me cry—my dad can't even come up with a way to make it seem better. He hugs me.

"Sorry." I got his shirt wet.

"And that's why they call me the Human Handkerchief." That makes me smile. "Can I interest you in a pizza run, Champ?"

"I think I'll just stay here, but thanks, Dad."

KAPUT, KAPISH?
(Translation: It's over, get it?)

Miracle: Nora's seat is empty on the bus. "Is your friend sick?" Gene asks.

"I hope not."

That sounds like we're still friends-ly enough...

Brooke is waiting for me in front of the school. "I wrote a new announcement!" She hands it to me.

It's so genius, I forget that I'm mad at her. Then Nora runs up and it all comes back to me. "My mom drove me." Nora's out of breath. "She didn't want the canned food sitting in the car until the Guide meeting."

"You probably already read this yesterday," I say to Nora, handing Brooke her paper, and the two of them look at each other.

"Actually, I showed you first," Brooke says.

Nora breaks the silence. "About yesterday—neither of us knew it was happening until Saturday—it was my mom's idea—and we were going to tell you Sunday, but—"

"But then Nora's mom got there early and—" Brooke adds.

"Here." Nora hands me a box of cold Rachel's cookies.

"Your mom should really make up her mind which one of us she wants you to be friends with." I can't believe I just said that. I have to walk away.

"I better get this announcement to Mr. Lovejoy," Brooke says. I walk faster, but I can hear the two of them right behind me.

"How about from now on, we tell each other everything?" Nora says to the back of my head.

"Mm." I was hoping for something more like "sorry."

Mr. Lovejoy nails Brooke's announcement: "I have an update on Farley's fourth annual Harvest Food Drive this morning. Pod 429 has offered to host a pizza party for the homeroom that collects the most cans. The pizza party winners will be announced the Tuesday before Thanksgiving!"

"And who doesn't love pizza?!" Mrs. Block says. "I'll ←NORA include a reminder for all of your parents in our newsletter."

After morning snack, I ask Mrs. B. if I can eat lunch in the room so I can do more research for the Town Meeting.

Do not mistake
silence for PEACE.

Mrs. B. is eating lunch at her desk. "Everything okay, Kate? I don't want to interrupt your research, but it was a rather unusual request. . . ."

"Sometimes I just like to be alone." not LEFT OUT.

She smiles a small smile. "Sometimes work is the easiest part of a school day. When people use the expression 'Growing old is not for sissies,' they're talking about old folks—a lot of them forget how hard it is being a kid. Growing *up* is not for sissies." She tosses her yogurt cup in the trash. "Two points! I've still got it!"

"You played basketball?"

"Captain and point guard for Munger Hill High School. Kate, if you're done there, could I get you to erase the whiteboard? Leave the band reminder up."

Specials

A Gym

B HEALTH

GYM INTERLUDE

MAC-CATWALK

MAC-ARABESQUE

ME CRUSHING on COLIN BEAM

Nora is at band before Brooke, Thomas, and me. Brooke and I take seats on either side of her. Brooke moves the stand over so I have to share with Nora. "Ew, what IS that?" Brooke asks.

(THAT)

Before Nora has a chance to answer, Mr. Bryant raises his stand and says, "As of today, we are six weeks away from our winter holiday concert. We work very hard in this room, but there are ten tiny two-letter words I want you to never forget: 'If it is to be, it is up to me.' And I'm not talking about our soloists; I am talking about the effort each one of you . . ."

Mr. B.-
IF IT
IS UP
TO US,
WE BE
ON IT!
....
HI, IF
AN EX
IS ME,
IT IS
SO ow.

"By the way, if there's a flute solo, you can have it," Nora whispers.

". . . and there are TWO flute solos; this time I remembered my co-leaders." Mr. Bryant could not possibly have heard Nora. "Please open your folders and take out 'Winter Wonderland.'"

"What IS this?" Brooke repeats her question. It's kind of obvious what it is; the real question is what is it doing there.

Nora sticks it under the stand. "It's my ABC gum. Rule #4: No gum in band?" No gum in school period (except during the state tests in the spring), plus Nora has a retainer, as in no gum ever, but that's beside the point.

FYDOY: you can make your own retainer out of a PAPER CLIP.

"Gross," Brooke says.

"Fine." Nora pops it back in her mouth. "What's he going to do? Kick me out? I'm moving."

"Everybody ready?" Mr. Bryant taps his stand. "Let's go valking in a vinter vonderland!"

I glance back and Eva smiles at me from the trumpet section. It's the first time I've felt like smiling all day. (Yesterday seems like approximately two hundred years ago.)

Eight measures in, Mr. Bryant stops the band. "We are *walking* in a winter wonderland—not running. Let's try that again!" Eight measures later: tap, tap, tap! "And again—we are *walking*, not meandering.

In a winter *wonderland*, not the town dump. Let me hear my flutes alone, brightly, please!"

On the third note, Nora's already-been-chewed gum gets stuck like a rubbery cork in her mouthpiece. She tries blowing it out. Then she sucks it in.

 "Everything okay, Nora?" Mr. Bryant asks. She swallows her gum, and her breathing goes back to normal. "Trumpets—let's have a nice big attack, not like Nora's—TA TA TA! Give me the first three notes. . . ."

Nora stays after to talk to Mr. Bryant. Brooke waits. And I wait, sort of like nothing ever happened between us.

"I told him I wanted you to play both solos," Nora says. "He said we should play them together."

SPOKEN LIKE SOMEONE
WHO HAS NEVER PLAYED with
I don't count so you can't too. NORA

Mr. Bryant

I can't think of anything nice to say; besides, there's no time for a conversation because we're late for Junior Guides.

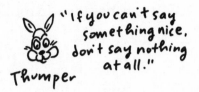

"If you can't say something nice, don't say nothing at all."

Thumper

We wait outside the cafetorium until the pod is finished reciting the Promise. "I don't get why everybody keeps promising the same thing over and over," Nora says. "A promise is a promise." Her voice is still froggy from choking.

"It's like the Pledge of Allegiance," Brooke says. Once again, I don't say anything, not that anyone notices.

"Hurry in, girls!" Mrs. Hallberg hands us spoons. "Grab a couple of pudding parfaits and take your seats."

Allie underlines Week 1. "Heather's morning announcement idea was super-smart."

FOOD DRIVE
WEEK 1
Heather*

Heather raises her hand. "Thank you! And Brooke built on my idea with the pizza contest."

"Almost sounds like it *was* her idea," Brooke whispers. "Wait, here comes the . . ."

I heard that.

Heather is famous for saying that and doing her squinty-eyes, even though she hasn't heard a thing.

"Week 1's total: twenty-four bags." Allie writes the 24 in red.

Eliza's hand shoots up. "If we use last year's estimate of fifteen pounds of food per bag, we have three hundred sixty pounds. And if we keep going at this rate, we should have a thousand eighty pounds on the last day, beating Pack 22's winning total last year by two hundred seventy-three pounds." Eliza loves math "more than pizza." (Real, not air quotes— she told me once.)

"Mind if I interrupt here?" I totally forgot to time Mrs. S. "I am pleased to officially announce we can all quit counting. The contest concept is kaput. I spoke with Mr. Landry. The Cub Scouts and the Junior Guides are going to pool our efforts (no pun intended!), and the good people at Luau Keys are more than happy to have all of us out for an afternoon of celebration at the completion of our food drive.

"Before I turn the reins back over to Allie, we have another leg of our harvest voyage to consider—our Thanksgiving baskets for the elderly.

eld·er·ly
Nice old

Yoda

"I have some more exciting news for you girls: this year, your baskets will be staying right here in town! Our town nurse helped me match each of you with one of our senior

REAL examples of
EXCITING NEWS:
1. We will be delivering
the baskets on alpaca-back.
2. Forget Luau Keys, we're
going to Disney!
3. Pod 429 has been
selected to taste-test
this year's fudge fun-raiser.

neighbors. Hmm?" She pauses. "I encourage you to reach out to your match right away, begin building a relationship. This will make for a much more meaningful journey."

Allie's turn. "Okay, wow," she says with a small *w*. "So now we're supposed to brainstorm some things we can put in our baskets." She writes *dinner*.

Faith says, "A Thanksgiving card." Everyone else's hand goes down. I'm trying to figure out which craft Mrs. Hallberg is setting up so I can add that to the list.

"Kleenex," Lily says. "My grandmother is always looking for Kleenex."

"My grandmother likes Puffs with aloe, not Kleenex," Faith chimes in.

"What about soap and gloves like we gave last year," I say. "Winter gloves, not rubber gloves."

"Terrific start," Mrs. S. interrupts again. "Although I didn't hear"—she switches to a whisper— "candles, and that's what we're making today! Okay, smocks, everyone!" Mrs. S. says in her regular voice.

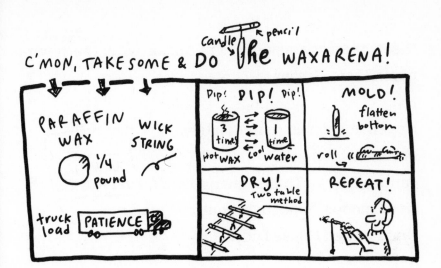

"Mrs. H. is going to hand out the matches while your candles are drying," Mrs. S. announces at 4:54.

Brooke's eyes are big. "We get to *light* them?!"

"Not matches-matches. She means the old people. You can't give an already-been-lit candle as a gift," says Nora (the girl who was choking on her already-been-chewed gum a half hour ago).

Mrs. H. hands Nora a folded paper. "No thank you, I'm moving," Nora says. Mrs. H. looks at Mrs. S. Nora goes on, "It's not a good idea to start building something if you're just going to have to tear it down. Or abandon it."

"Keep that one aside; I will speak with the town nurse," Mrs. S. says.

I open my paper immediately. My stomach flips.

Edie Verlangen
122 Pugh Road

Nora snoops. "Ooooooh, you got the Haunted House Lady."

"Mrs. Staughton, are you *sure* these people *want* visitors?" I ask.

"In every case." Mrs. Staughton nods way too many times. "In fact, we have more senior requests than we have Guides to fill them. Mr. Landry agreed to have Pack 22 take on the rest of the list." With that, Mrs. Staughton vanishes in a cloud of smoke.

Pssssssssshhhht. "First time for everything!" Mrs. S. smiles, replacing the cap on her red can.

"Deodorant?" Brooke whispers.

"Fire extinguisher. Handheld. Our wax was on fire!"
Mrs. S. zips up her fanny pack and gives it a couple
congratulatory pats.

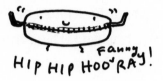

HIP HIP HOO'RAY!

PHONE-y

"How was the meeting?" Mom asks, sprinkling cheese on her taco at the kitchen island. Fern and I are already at the table. I gave her ten olive slices, which she puts on her fingertips and then eats one by one.

"We're all ears, Champ." My dad is holding taco shells on either side of his head.

"Fern, stop laughing," Mom says. "You're encouraging him."

"We're not delivering baskets to the elderly at Apple Valley this year. Mrs. Staughton—"

"She can't get rid of that—it's a tradition!" Robin looks at my mom.

"She's not. She had the town nurse match us up with elderly neighbors.

Things I'll miss about
APPLE VALLEY SENIOR CENTER

1. Stopping at the Qwik Mart on the way there
2. The desserts
3. Having Brooke with me

I have Mrs. Verlangen." Mom looks at Dad. "I'm supposed to get to know her right away so I can make her basket more . . . personal."

"You can give her a call after we finish up here," Mom says.

"Isn't it kind of late for the elderly—?"

"We call your Grammalolo after dinner. It's the only time we're all home."

"But Grammalolo isn't elderly, she's—"

"Grumpy," Fern says, and my dad tries not to laugh.

"Can we skip Bob tonight, Dad?" I ask. "I want to make my call."

"Sure thing, Champ. Let's see what we're skipping. . . ."
He throws it back in.

Not everything that can be counted counts, and not everything that counts can be counted.
—William Bruce Cameron

REHEARS-A-CALL

TAKE 1

"DIAL TONE" Yes, um, hello, HI, Mrs. Verlangen? Would you be interested in hanging— No.

TAKE 2

Hello, Mrs. Verlangen, you don't know me but I need to find out some personal "DIAL" TONE inform—ACK.

My hand is on the phone, about to make my call, when it rings.

"Hi, it's me, Brooke. I just wanted to say I noticed . . . that you weren't saying anything. And I don't know what to say, besides I'm sorry." It's quiet, and then she adds, "There wasn't even anything fun or funny that happened when Nora and I were playing *our* duets."

It was my turn to not know what to say. Brooke went on. "I'm not very good at having—at being best friends with more than one person." (Throat clear.) "Yeah, so, sorry."

"Thanks." There are a few seconds of silence. "Well, I'm supposed to call my elderly person, so I better go now."

"I think I'll do that tomorrow," Brooke says. "You're better than me at phone calls."

"Thanks." Before I hang up, I say, "I'll let you know how it goes."

I don't even put the phone down, just dial, and Mrs. Verlangen picks up, first ring.

"Hello, Mrs. Verlangen. This is Kate Geller calling. Is this a bad time?"

"This is a fine time, Kate Geller." She hesitates. "As far as I know."

"I am making you a Thanksgiving basket in Junior Guides, and I think I could make a better basket if I knew you better."

Maybe the Butter BattleBook would make your basket better. (or a rubber baby buggy bumper)

"This is an interview, then, is it?"

"An interview? Oh. No. I was hoping I could come for a visit."

"Inviting yourself for a visit." She laughs.

". . . We could meet somewhere."

"Never mind, I'm making this difficult, Kate Geller. What are you doing tomorrow at four?"

Four's too spoo—dark. "How about three-thirty? I should really be home before—"

"I have tea at four. I'll leave the door unlocked. You can let yourself in."

LATER THAT NIGHT . . .

SUPER helpful CHICKEN

Dad is putting Fern to bed. Mom is in her office. "Mom, I'm having tea with Mrs. Verlangen tomorrow."

"One second." She finishes typing something, then turns to me. "That's wonderful. Wear something nice." She reaches into the front of her bottom right-hand desk drawer and hands me a tin of shortbread. "Bring these with you."

MOM'S "SECRET" SNACK STASH

"What else do you have in there?"

She laughs. "Never mind. Isn't it your bedtime?" *Translation*: Run along. Scoot. Skedaddle.

I get into my pj's, close my bunk curtains, and remove my clipboard from the slats over my head.

INTERVIEW
1. Who is your fave President?
2. What is your fave snack food?
3.

"Mind if I butt in?" I'm looking at Robin's pajama bottoms. "What're you working on—I'm dying to know, what did you think?" *What did I think* . . . "About Will?" Robin is all smiley. "He really likes you."

Go. big LITTLE SISTER!

"Will? Yeah, I mean, he's really nice, and definitely a really good kiss— I mean sleeper. . . ."

"Very funny."

"I thought you said 'crush.' He's like . . . like a boyfriend."

"Do you think Mom knows, the way she was asking about him?"

"You mean the way I answered? Sorry, all of a sudden, I didn't know how much she wasn't supposed to know and—"

"I'll tell them, Kate—I'm just not ready yet." She sighs. "Everything's so much easier for you. I'm sick of being the oldest, the first with everything."

"Everything is *not* so easy. Tuesday afternoon was the Worst Afternoon Ever."

"We didn't really care that you were spying." She puts her arm around me.

"Not that." Robin takes her arm back. "Eva and I saw Brooke and Nora together at the mall. They were planning on being together the whole time—they just weren't planning on being seen by us . . . well, me."

"You do stuff with Brooke alone or Nora alone—"

"I don't lie about it! I was sure Brooke was feeling left out—"

"Have they apologized?"

have/will never admit^ted out loud ↘

I put my head on her shoulder. I am getting sleepy. "Brooke apologized tonight. It doesn't automatically make everything better. Why am I the one who always has to understand what it's like to be everybody else?"

"You're good at it." She smiles. "Put your head on your pillow." She turns off the light and does a lying-down egg thing. I'm asleep before the imaginary whites touch my ears.

LINGON BERRY MUCH

Brooke is waiting in the bus circle. "How'd it go?"

"How'd *what* go?!" Nora stops walking. "I thought we were telling each other everything."

"Brooke's asking about my elderly person phone call. It's not a secret or anything," I say. "We're having tea at her house this afternoon."

"By yourself?" Brooke asks.

ALONE, I CAN!!

"I'll go with you," Nora offers.

"Thanks, but I think I better go alone."

We check the food drive cartons on the way to our lockers. The Kapizza Kontest is totally working. All the cartons are practically full after one day. Mrs. Block is rearranging 5B's collection. "I don't know why I bother with extra credit and bonus recess—you all do your best work for pizza. Do you

122

have a plan to empty these out?" Mrs. Block looks at Brooke and Thomas, who are hovering.

"We do," Brooke says.

WE DO?!.?!.?!.?!.

We do?

It's in... formation.

Yes, we have some information, which we'll give you after...

We think of it?

after lunch!

Brooke and I look for Allie at lunch. "That seat's saved for Allie," Heather says, as if we were going to take it.

"Perfect. We need to talk to her," Brooke says.

"About?"

ABOUT how we can't talk to HER unless we tell YOU what it's ABOUT.

"Canned food drive."

"Actually, about storage space," I say as Allie walks over.

"Allie, you need to ask Mr. Lovejoy where we can store the cans. There," Heather says. "You can go back to your regular table."

Mrs. B. reminds us at the beginning of social studies that the Town Meeting is only a week away. In the first four minutes, Peter Buttrick gets two questions wrong.

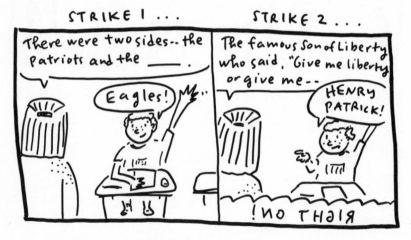

I'm not even on the bus when Nora starts talking to me. "You'll probably say no, which is why I never ask—I'll just get it over with. . . . Can you come over . . . today?"

"I can't."

"What do I have to do to get you to stop being mad at me?"

"I'm having tea with Mrs. Verlangen."

"Doh." Nora shook her head. A while later, she asks, "What do you think you'll talk about, anyway?"

"Not sure. But I already know one thing I can put in her Thanksgiving basket."

"I'll be with you in five!" Dad yells when he hears my backpack drop on the kitchen floor. Rocky runs in.

"Four! Three! Two!" Sometimes I can get Rocky going with a countdown.

"Mom said to make sure you aren't wearing anything ratty. And I was thinking it's probably a good idea to take Mrs. Verlangen a little something," he says. "I had these in my office."

MEGA·BAG!

"Thanks, Dad." I hide the Cracker Jacks in my desk drawer and tie the purple ribbon I used to wear as a headband around the shortbread tin Mom gave me last night. After I skim my interview questions, I slide them in my pocket, mostly for good luck.

"Will I want to go back?"
I turn my K8 ball upside down.
"Not necessary, thanks."

ASK AGAIN LATER

K8

I'm not sure if you're supposed to knock before you "let yourself in," but I do. And forget what I said about Mrs. Verlangen earlier—she *could* get to the door in a hurry if she wanted to. Backwards.

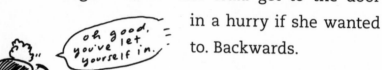

oh good, you've let yourself in.

"This hallway is a nuisance." I would feel a lot more comfortable if I could see her face. "Too narrow." The hallway could also use a light, and fewer cobwebs. I follow her into her kitchen, and she turns around. "Now, let me have a look at you. And vice versa, I suppose."

As Mr. Lovejoy says, "You only get one first impression." Mrs. Verlangen looks like the antonym for scary. She kind of reminds me of Stuart Little, driving the sports car.

I hand her the tin. "These are for you."

"Well, Kate Geller, I see we already have one thing in common!"

POSSIBLE THINGS
in COMMON
1. We both live on Pugh Rd.
2. We are both female mammals.
3. Two eyes, two ears, two arms, etc.

"Purple is also my favorite color," she says. I smile, even though purple was my favorite color in second grade. It's good basket information.

Mrs. Verlangen does not need any help serving tea. She sets the pot on the table and spreads a small napkin across her lap. "Before you sit down, Kate, see if you can reach that jar of lingonberry jam." I hand it to her and try not to snoop at all the other things on her shelves. "I have to keep it where it's hard to get, or I'd be at it all the time."

We each make a small pool of jam on our plates and spread it on the shortbread. She dunks hers in her tea and scoops up the floaters with her spoon.

It's obvious you're not drinking me.

Ummmm-one-thousand, two-one-thousand . . . "Have you really lived here for fifty years?"

"Fifty-two," she answers. "That's a long time." A white cat twice the size of her lap lands on her napkin. "Verdi! You just used up one of my lives!" She looks him in his green eyes. "Verdi, this is Kate. He usually makes himself scarce when I have company. He's had to sit through all of my stories at least once."

TMI

"Rocky knows all my stories, too," I say. "He's my dog."

(Rocky and I have sleep-unders.)

Mrs. Verlangen's pats flatten Verdi's ears. I can hear his purring. "Best friends, aren't they?"

"I actually have two best friends—Brooke and Nora."

"Mr. Verlangen was my best friend."

As in best dead friend. I'm afraid she's going to cry, so I look at my watch. "I better go, it's after four-thirty, and I haven't started my homework."

"Do they give you much in fifth grade?" Her eyes are shiny, not watery at all.

I only have fourth (and third and second and first) grade to compare it to. "Pretty much."

She tells me a few more stories, and when she's finished, she says, "Be a dear and put these in the sink." She hands me her cup and plate, and then her lingonberry jam. "Rummage around in the back there, see if you can find any cans—I saw you girls out collecting for your contest." I find four ant traps, a couple of cans of pumpkin, and some Michigan cherries. "Relics from my pie-baking days," Mrs. Verlangen says when she sees them.

note to self

CHECK
FRESHNESS
DATE

For some reason, I say, "It's actually not a contest, well, it is, but . . ." and I explain the whole thing to her, beginning with how Mrs. Lawrence, our old Junior Guide leader, used to do everything.

"I don't know why some people insist on making improvements where none are necessary—but it sounds like Mrs. Staughton's made a few things better. If not for her, the two of us wouldn't be talking. Don't let me keep you; it's after five o'clock now, Kate."

"Thank you very much for the cans, and the tea," which might be the best cup of tea I ever tasted. (Also the second cup of tea I ever tasted.)

"You're very welcome, Kate." Mrs. Verlangen scooter-walks me to the door, facing forward. She waves. I guess we could have shaken hands or something. "Verdi and I have tea every day at four," she calls after me. "You're welcome to join us anytime—bring your own beverage if my tea doesn't suit you."

why I RUN HOME

Happy 50% / 36% Relieved / 14% It's dark.

"I was getting ready to come after you," my dad says when I walk in. "I was afraid Mrs. Verlangen was holding you hostage until you finished your tea."

"What's she like?" Robin comes into the kitchen, and my mom is right behind her.

"She invited me back. She's . . ." It's hard to say what someone's like when you've never known anyone else like her. "Not what I expected. I mean she's eighty-four, but you forget she's old when she's talking.

"She was born in Austria, but she's lived here since she was eleven. Well, not *here*, New York, and then here. And she said I could join her and Verdi for tea anytime."

"Verdi takes care of her?"

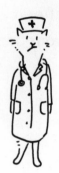

I would have laughed harder if I wasn't the only one who got the joke. "Verdi is her cat. They take care of each other."

"Maybe she would like to come here for tea sometime," Mom suggests.

I don't see how, but I say, "Maybe."

OUR HOUSE

SPEED MEETING

Allie calls an Emergency Meeting by the drink machines (a.k.a. where Nora sits) at lunch. "Starting Monday, Mr. Lovejoy wants us to collect the cans from all the classrooms and put them in the closet by the nurse's office. Mrs. McGee complained that she was up to her earlobes in cans."

Are the cans
UP to
~ OR ~
are
Mrs. McGEE's
EARLOBES

DOWN to the cans?
FACT: your earlobes never stop growing.

"We'll take turns—our usual pairs, and you three can go together," Allie says, looking at Brooke, Nora, and me. "Eliza will make up a schedule. Meeting dismissed."

"Meeting dismissed," Nora repeats to Brooke and me. "You can go back to your normal table." Brooke empties her lunch bag on Nora's table. Nora spreads out her lunch and looks up at Brooke. "This side's really better. You can see everyone from here." Brooke pushes her food across the table and sits next to Nora. I sit on the other side of Brooke.

"Looks like Pack 22 is having an emergency meeting," Brooke says.

"Yeah, they really put the zero in col-lab-0-ra-tion," I say. Neither of them laughs, but it's starting to feel like we're friends again.

PACK 22'S "EMERGENCY MEETING"

Mrs. Block is at the door when we come in from lunch recess. *Translation:* She is super-excited about social studies. "Everybody, assume your Town Hall identities and get ready for a round of Revolutionary Speed Dating. I will give you a study topic, and you will have five minutes to discuss it with the person sitting across from you. When the bell rings"—she clangs the bell—"those of you on my right will move one desk to your left and we'll *clang* do it again! Now take a moment to introduce yourselves."

"Rebecca Best." Hui Zong holds out her hand.

"Hannah . . ." *Last name, Hannah?* "Renner." We shake.

ALSO a palindrome - Nice!

"First topic," Mrs. B. announces. "French and Indian wars, 1754 to 1763. Who can give us a speed-summary before we get started?"

Thomas Bergen volunteers. "The British, the Iroquois Indians, and the English colonists fought against the French, the Algonquin Indians, and the French colonists for more land in North America."

"Thank you, Thomas. Begin your five minutes."

"This was the King's idea," Rebecca begins. "I'm sure he thought it was a good one—he won. But now he's making us pay for it. And it cost quite a lot. Nearly cost me Mr. Best."

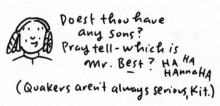
Doest thou have any sons?
Pray tell - which is mr. Best? HA HA HAnnaHA
(Quakers aren't always serious, Kit.)

"Thou wast lucky thou's husband was spared. The price of a single life costeth too much," I say in colonial-ish.

"Time!" Mrs. Block rings her bell. Eliza, a.k.a. Patience Clay, moves over in front of me. "New topic:

135

Proclamation of 1763, which is . . . anybody? Besides Thomas?"

I raise my hand. "The king told the colonists they could not go west so they would not get into more fights with the Indians."

The bell rings again. "Next date—introduce yourselves!"

Awkward!!!

Did she HAVE to say DATE?!

Colin, a.k.a. Harry Coombs, puts out his hand and I/Hannah shake it. "Your topic is the Sugar Act of 1764. Two sentences on the Sugar Act?"

It's some tax that the colonists had to pay on sugar—I can't concentrate. I can still feel Colin's sweat on

PORTRAIT of my HAND WITH COLIN'S HAND SWEAT

my hand. "You go first," Colin says.

I have no idea whose side Colin/Harry is on. "This tax is bad for business—no offense-eth—"

"Are you in the alcohol, er, spirits business? Or are you a cake boss—baker?"

Is he joking? "I am a seamstress."

"This tax is fair and nutritious. . . ."

"The King gives us nothing for our taxes—"

"The King defends your land, and you expect to pay him nothing?" BELL!

"Did you notice the only time Mrs. B. called it a date was when I was with Colin," I point out to Brooke on our way to the buses.

"Do you, Kate Hannah Renner Geller, take Colin and his Hairy Combs to be your husband—?"

THOUGHT
BUBBLES

THEN:

Having a
new friend
is easier than
dealing with
two old ones.

& NOW:

- POP! -

"Ew! Stop it!" I push her away.

"Just kidding," Brooke says. "Want to come over tomorrow?"

I do, but . . . "I am going to the Paysons' to play basketball." It's not like last time. This time it was

137

my idea. Basketball tryouts are on Monday, as in three days from now.

"Is it okay if I have Nora over?" she asks.

S is for the 7,000 ways it is NOT okay.
U**R** just kidding, right?
Eʰ! the End.

TOP ~~CHEF~~ SECRET

Mom drops us off at the Paysons' on Saturday morning, and Robin and Grace go out for a run.

"Is Will sleeping?" I ask Eva on the way up to her room.

"Working."

"Here, I made us these." I hand Eva a Terrible Spy Club membership card and a free gift.

T.S.C.
INVISIBLE INK PEN
FREE with
membership
~~Sharpie~~
WORKS only WITH
EYES CLOSED!

"Let me put it someplace top secret," she says, and sticks the card up in the middle of her bulletin board. "Basketball?"

We're doing left-hand dribble for the world's longest five minutes. "Does Thomas Bergen ever talk to you in band?" I ask, since they sit next to each other.

"About what?" Eva asks.

"About anything. He never talks to Brooke or me."

"He's actually nice. I wish I could play the trumpet like him."

"Wait, do you have a crush on him?"

"No, we're friends!" It's her turn to dribble the ball on her foot.

"Heads up!" I yell. Will is pulling into the driveway.

"Stop, don't shoot! Innocent brother coming through!" Will steals Eva's ball and makes a layup. "One-handed!" (His other hand is full.)

"What's in the bag?" Eva asks.

"Let me look." Will opens the bag. "Let's see, it's . . . it's . . . none of your business!" Groan. "It's a present for your sister, Kate. A surprise—you two have to promise not to tell."

We nod. "Wet pinky promise?" Will says.

"Gross, Will!" Eva pushes his hand away.

 "Wow, they're cool!" we both say.

"Jinx, you owe me a Sprite!" Eva says.

"How'd you know her size?" I ask Will.

"I checked out the ones she's wearing."

"Ooh, you're brave," I say, holding my nose.

"Robin told me you were funny." Will smiles and puts the shoes back in the bag. "You two must be getting hungry. Beave, why don't you challenge your friend to a round of Top Chef?"

It has to be an improvement over going to the mall. "Explain how it works," Will tells Eva as he holds the door for us.

EVA aka
_____
Beave
M.P. (Molly's Pal)
Lil Bit
Bitty
Bitsy
It Girl

"You have ten minutes to come up with the best lunch using anything you find in the kitchen. And you make five portions. Two for us, plus the judges. I'm pretty sure my mom and dad won't want any," Eva says.

"Okay, but I have no idea what's in your refrigerator."

"Trust me, neither do I." She opens the fridge and a bag of soft tortillas falls on the floor. I grab it.

"It's a sign!" I say.

"I've got the timer, and I'll round up your judges," Will offers. "Ten minutes—on your marks, get set, go!" We race around the kitchen without bumping into each other. Then, with three minutes and eleven seconds left, Eva puts something in the oven.

"Wait, you're allowed to use the oven?"

"I said anything in the kitchen," she says.

I sprinkle pomegranate seeds on the last of the five plates just as the timer goes off.

Robin and Grace are sitting on either side of Will. We present our plates.

The KATE-ILLA

Soft flour tortilla filled with hummus, cheddar, and apple- topped with mayo- hot sauce + pomegranate

EVA'S "AWESOMELETTE"

Basically eggs, goat cheese + green onions

The judges talk quietly, and then the three of them push their Kate-illas toward us. "Come on—you're kidding!" Eva exclaims.

"Top chef—Kate Geller!" Grace says. Eva throws down her oven mitt.

"And, wait—the sportsmanship award ALSO goes
to . . . Kate Geller!" The three of
them say my name together.

con·ge·ni·al·i·ty
Friendliness

root word:
Gene

a ka
Miss/Ms./Mrs./Mr.
CONGENIALITY

Molly comes racing in. "No leftovers, boy." Molly is
still looking up at Eva. She pats him between the
eyes. "I know, I'm a bad loser, but I bounce back fast,
right?"

I'd admit I'm the same way, but . . .

As long as I keep winning,
I'll never have to :)

Will drives Robin and me home. Grammalolo is in
the kitchen.

"To what or whom do I owe this special appearance?"
she says to Robin. (Robin is usually absent for
Saturday dinners.)

144

my boyfriend, WILL,
just dropped me off.

The Wallaces and
the Ramirezes —
No babysitting tonight!

Robin hugs Grammalolo, then goes up to her room. I follow her. "I think Grammalolo would really like Will."

"She'll meet him at Thanksgiving."

"You're waiting until Thanksgiving?! You never said this secret was going to last *that* long."

"Kate, that's less than two weeks away! Look, I want to be able to keep training at the Paysons'. It's been really good for me and Grace . . . and Will. Please?" Robin says. "Besides, Mom and Dad keep stuff from us all the time."

"And that drives me crazy!"

"Hey, look what Will gave me for race day," Robin says, which isn't technically changing the subject.

"He showed us in the driveway. They're secret, too, right?" I go to my room to get the checkbook cover I made for Grammalolo.

"It's exactly what I ordered," Grammalolo says. I wait. Her honest opinion (*Translation:* burn) usually comes next. "How are you making out*with your social studies project?"

* On page 497!

"I've been trying to follow your advice, you know, about joining the forces—the Patriots—without using force. One question: what if I join and someone on King George's side gets hurt or killed by mistake?"

Grammalolo stays for family movie night. "I love how Mrs. McGillicutty insists we watch *Up*, and then she is *down* for the count," she laughs as my dad carries Fern upstairs. "Well, I guess it's everybody's bedtime. I'll see myself to the door."

Before Mom can finish saying, "Let me turn on some—" Grammalolo trips. Mom catches her. I catch my breath.

G·LoLo	G·Force (gravity)
1	0

Robin gets the lights.

"Thank you, dear, and tell those babies you're sitting on that they get to see you more than your grandmother does. I'm not getting any younger."

"You okay, Mom? Can I drive you home?" My mother looks worried.

"I'm fine," Grammalolo says. "Perfectly fine." And she disappears down the walk.

The NEW BROOKE

"Wait'll you see Brooke's new glasses," Nora says when I sit down on the bus.

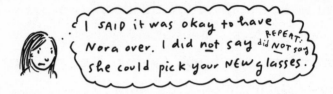

"And her haircut!"

At first, when I get off the bus, I literally don't *see*. I don't recognize my best friend in her new glasses and hair until she says hi, at which point I stop in my tracks and cause a huge pileup behind me.

"You look so much older!" Nora says behind me, nudging me forward.

"Yeah, definitely," I say, swallowing.

"I can still put my hair in braids," Brooke says. And I wish she would, right this instant, and at least give me some time to get used to the idea. Everyone else seems fine; I mean, they seem to like the new look.

 "I have an important announcement to make regarding our canned food drive. Mrs. Staughton, substitute by day, super Junior Guide leader by afternoon, has proposed that the price of admission to next week's pep rally be one or more cans of food. If Farley families donate over 1,000 cans of food, the Farley faculty, including yours truly, will dance the cancan." Brooke looks for me, and I actually look away. I don't want her to think I've been staring. "One, or more, cans of food, if you wish to attend the all-school homecoming pep rally in the gym next Tuesday."

"That's our super-dee-duper Junior Guide leader," Brooke says, like she would have with her old look.

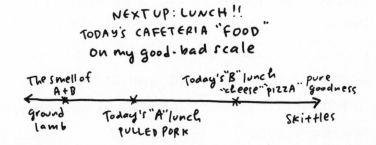

Eva stops at our table on the way to hers at lunch. "Wow, Brooke! At first I thought you were a new girl," she says. "I really like your hair."

"Thanks." Brooke blushes.

"I'll wait for you in the lobby after school," Eva says to me. "I think we're the only fifth graders trying out, except Heather." Heather doesn't count; she's played on the 5/6-grade basketball team since she was in third grade.

"Good luck," Brooke calls after Eva, then turns to me. "I didn't know tryouts were today." *And I didn't know you were getting a complete makeover.*

yes, we are best friends.

No, we didn't just find each other on the Internet.

wish me luck or
Brooke doesn't wait for me at dismissal. I can see Eva at the end of the hall. She's already in her basketball clothes. "Ms. Crowley let me get changed during pack-up time. Um, you know what I said to Brooke before—I actually think I like her braids better, don't you?"

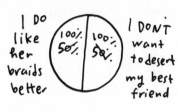

Yes, I don't...
DESERT-PIE CHART

I DO like her braids better | 100% 50% | 100% 50% | I DON'T want to desert my best friend

"It's just what we're used to. She had to get rid of them sometime—no one wears braids in high school."

It turns out you don't need luck*to be on Coach Vic's team. "Coach Vic runs a no-cut team." (Coach Vic refers to himself as Coach Vic.) "Vic is short for Victor, as in winner. Coach Vic can make a winner out of every one of you girls, as long as you're willing to H-U-S-T-L-E. Now, who wants the ball?" Eva and I raise our hands. Heather takes the ball. "If your hands are raised, keep them up nice and high—now you six give me two down-and-backs, go!" *Is he serious?* "GO!"

*EXCEPT YOU DON'T WANT to BE in the FRONT ROW for FOOT FIRE.

COACH VIC
Unfortunate
(THe REAR VIEW)

"Lesson #1: If you want the ball, you take the ball. You are going to learn to be A-G-G-R-E-S-S-I-V-E"—and S-P-E-L-L—"with Coach Vic."

Eva and I are changing out of our basketball shoes after practice. "Welcome to the team," Heather says as she's walking out of the gym with two of the sixth graders.

(PRIVATE)
ZING-SHOT
eah, if I'd known there were no cuts, I would've tried out in third grade, too.

Eva rolls her eyes. "I don't like her," she says.

"I'm not so sure about Coach V-I-C, either," I say. Eva knits her eyebrows into a question mark. (Not literally.) "Never mind," I say. I guess friends don't have to have *everything* in common. Eva and I have basketball. Brooke has my sense of humor. *And new hair and glasses.*

"What's for dinner?" I ask my dad.

Drumroll: "Meatloaf."

COMPOUND
I am so hungry, it's hard to believe that one word could ruin my appetite.

My dad's recipe for meatloaf = meat in a loaf pan. Zero points for creativity, −5,000 points for taste.

I transfer forkfuls of meatloaf from my plate to my napkin to Rocky, but he's only good for five. "Not hungry, Champ?" my dad says, eyeing my leftovers.

"It's not her favorite," my mom answers for me. Please note: she has leftovers, too. "Adam, Kate made the basketball team!"

"And you waited till now to tell me?!" Dad says. "Congratulations! How do you like Coach Vic?"

"Uh, he's . . . weird."

"Coach Vic is the winningest coach in Farley's history," Dad says.

"I think Kate means he'll take some getting used to," Mom translates for me.

"Coach Vic is W-E-I-R-D," Robin says. "Does he still S-P-E-L-L everything?"

"Bob thanks you for that wonderful segue. How did everyone do?"

pronounced

se·gue
Lead-in

Segway

The only normal people are the ones you don't know very well.
—Joe Ancis

"I am in total agreement with your friend Joe. I've realized it's hard enough to figure out what works for me and my family—I've got no business judging others," Mom says.

"It kind of made me think the opposite, not that I don't agree with Mom, or Joe," I begin awkwardly. "But I think the only *weird* people are the ones you don't know very well. Everybody thinks Mrs. Verlangen is weird. She's really not."

"Well put, Kate!" My dad and mom exchange smiles. "And what's normal, anyway? Boring."

FERNish for "No offense."

"This is boring," Fern pipes up. "On the fence."

"Fine, I'll pick another one." Dad closes his eyes and swirls the papers around. "This is your mother's writing."

A sister can be seen as someone who is both ourselves and very much not ourselves — a special kind of double.
—Toni Morrison

AFTER·SCHOOL SPECIAL

My dad has his coat on when I get home from school.

"I'm going to run out to Acme Sports and pick up a pair of sneakers for Robin's race day. Mom's idea— what's that face, Kattila? You need a snack first?"

Eliminates ideas instantly!

"I hate Acme Sports. Besides, don't you need Robin's feet to buy her sneakers?"

"They're a surprise, and that's why we're giving them to her a week ahead of time."

"Hey, would you mind dropping me at Mrs. Verlangen's on the way?"

"Is she expecting you?"

"I won't stay long."

"After you." My dad holds the door.

RING and WAIT... and WAIT... and WAIT... and

My dad honks, and I give one last knock, then jog to the car.

"Kate Geller, is that you?" Mrs. Verlangen calls from the door, and I sprint back.

"Sorry, next time I'll call first."

"Come in, I'm not dressed for outdoors." Mrs. V. is in her bathrobe. "Or indoors," she laughs. She's using a walker, which explains what took her so long. "I was in the bedroom, and my scooter-pal is in the kitchen. The doctor wants me to get more exercise. What a bore. Now, Kate, tell me what's going on in your world. . . ."

Mrs. V. and I have a lot of catching up to do, basically our whole lives, but I spend the next ten minutes filling her in on the last five days.

She summarizes, "Nora's still Nora. Brooke may still be Brooke, but she doesn't have her braids anymore. And you've made the basketball team (congratulations), with your new friend Eva. It can be difficult sometimes, can't it, having two best friends." I nod. I don't want her to see *me* cry. "Or maybe it's having the one 'best' friend that is difficult. Different friends can be the best at different things. My sister Violet was like my twin. And Pansy

PANSY "Pickle" GHERKIN ♥

Gherkin—her name alone could set me to laughing." Which it did, just then. "Care for a biscuit?" She shook my finger. "You know where I keep the jam." I fix us each a biscuit.

"Before I forget, push that scooter over here—I've found you a very special can." I set the scooter beside her. She plops herself on, then rips down the hall and opens the front door. "See it there?" she says, pointing to the corner of the garage. "Look at the expiration date!" she calls once I have it in my hands.

EXP: MAR 1979

"Could make a grand finale!" Mrs. V. makes an exploding noise, and her fingers flutter down to her lap. "Of course, botulism is no laughing matter," she says once we both stop laughing.

bot·u·lism
Poisoning caused by bad canned food

"I better go." I give her a hug. "I promised my dad it would be a quick visit."

"Where are you taking that can?"

"Very far away," I say, closing the door behind me.

The new sneakers do not come out at dinner. There's still a very small chance this could all work out. It's way past my bedtime. I silent-walk down the hall. Robin is doing her homework at her desk. "Rob," I say, mostly so I don't scare her.

= very small =
= SLIM = FAT =
CHANCE
no

"What's up, Kate?"

"Me." Robin raises her eyebrows. "I can't get to sleep." She puts her pencil down and swivels so she's facing me. "You *have* to tell Mom and Dad about Will."

"Gee, thanks for the daily reminder—"

I have no choice. "They bought you new sneakers today—a surprise—for race day."

"Ohhh." She takes her hair out, twists it, and puts it back up again. I can tell she's thinking about it.

"They'd really like him," I say.

"That's part of the problem. I'm not ready to share him with . . . with them. Thanks for telling me." She stands up and squeezes my shoulders. "Don't look so worried. I'll come up with something. Hey, how are things with Brooke and Nora?"

"I hope you're not trying to make me feel less worried." She's waiting for my answer. "They're not bad—oh, I don't know. Maybe *that's* the worst part. I really don't know. I'm starting to wonder if Nora and I were ever friends. . . . There's a difference between being friendly to someone and—and I'm not sure I even know Brooke anymore."

"Because she got new glasses and a haircut? C'mon, Kate—she's still the same person—"

"Maybe the new hair and the glasses *are* who she is."

"People change, friendships change—Olivia Turek and I were BFFs when I was your age, and now we say hi to each other but . . ."

"Okay, this is really NOT making me feel better. I capital-H-hate change."

"Capital-H-heartily dislike."
(There's a rule against hating

Banned
at school
+ home

synonyms:
1. abhor
2. deplore
3. detest
4. loathe

in our house.) "Things would get pretty boring if they always stayed the same."

"Wrong. If things stayed the same, you wouldn't waste time worrying and you could read, or learn to do fishtail braids . . ."

"Or sleep. I don't want to sound like Dad, but a good night's sleep makes a big difference." She walks me back to my room.

"Rob, will you lie here for just a second?" It's a really little-sisterish question, but she pretends not to notice and tucks us both in.

TGIF (Too gross it's F. day)

mrs. P. flossing
at desk

2 GOOD
+2 B
4 GOTTEN

We are actually *early* to art. After attendance, Mrs. Petty announces, "I am going to have you watch a YouTube video while I pass out your paper and quill pens."

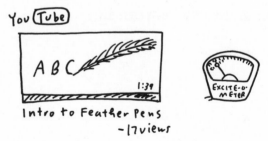

You Tube

A B C

1:39

Intro to Feather Pens
—17 views

EXCITE-O-METER

"Today, obviously, you will be practicing your calligraphy. Why do you think I'm having you write this sentence?" She points to her TV.

The quick brown fox jumps over the lazy dog.

MRS. P. T.V.

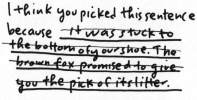

I think you picked this sentence because ~~it was stuck to the bottom of your shoe. The brown fox promised to give you the pick of its litter.~~

I SPY FLOSS

Eliza raises her hand.

Brooke snorts. She is obviously thinking of something even funnier than I am. Oh, never mind—I spy with my little eye the snort-source. Mrs. Petty calls on Eliza. "Because it has all the letters of the alphabet."

"Precisely." Mrs. P. smiles. "If anybody needs a review of last week's lesson, please see me. Otherwise, you may begin."

The crazy pub dog jaws of Waxmen's quirky luv?♥♥♥

The frown box

Excuse the interruption. Band members, please report to the music room at this time.

"Band members' papers, please!" Mrs. Petty holds out her hand. I slide my paper under Brooke's. "You three may go ahead. Tell Mr. Bryant that Kate will be along after she finishes writing the correct practice sentence."

"But—it is—it uses—I was just trying to come up with something a little more—" Her face is frozen. "Never mind." I write the fox sentence and turn it in.

"We do what we're asked *first*, Kate, and then, *if* and *when* we have time . . ." *Speaking of time, Mrs. Petty, gotta run.*

I slip into the seat next to Brooke, put my flute together, and start playing without Mr. Bryant ever stopping the band. Brooke is really swaying to the music. She practically takes me out with her right elbow. I don't remember her ever playing t^h$_i$s w^{a}y, but maybe it's part of her new look. And then, I spy with my close-up eye . . .

At the first rest, I whisper, "How—?!"

"Eliza didn't even know it was there!" She picks the Petty-floss off her sleeve, whips it toward me, then pockets it.

"Paus-a!" Mr. Bryant stops everyone. "Not bad for a first pass, my little nutcrackers. That concludes the March—Kate, you missed the solo, but we'll be revisiting it. Let's take out 'Waltz of the Flowers' next. . . ."

"How'd the solo go?" I ask Nora on our way to Guides.

"She told him to wait for you," Brooke answers.

"Excuse me—I can answer for myself," Nora grumbles. "Basically, what *she* said. I am not ready for a sight-reading solo."

"See ya, Kate!" I turn around, and Eva's waving.

"Why isn't she in Guides?" Nora asks.

I shrug. The topic has never come up.

Mrs. Staughton hands us the snack container and a big orange plate as we walk into the cafetorium. "Put some of these down first." She has a pile of fake oak leaves. "And then arrange the snack on top. Please. Girls."

Brooke and I leaf the plate, and Nora sets the snacks out. Mrs. S. watches the entire time. "What?" Nora says. "I'm putting all the cotton balls facing in."

"Those are acorns. Acorns strewn across a forest floor," Mrs. S. says, rearranging them. "They *are* a bit top-heavy." She unzips her fanny pack and  extracts a tiny jar of peanut butter. "A little dab, like glue—there, they won't give you any more trouble."

This is Allie's last meeting as pod president. (It's Eliza's turn in December.) Once again, it's time to play

Guess-How-Long-Before . . . but I can't get Brooke's attention. She and Nora are too busy laughing about _no clue_.

"If I had known we could use our neighborhood's cans for the pizza contest"—Heather is standing (*Translation:* making a speech)—"like Kate did, I never would have turned mine in to the pod."

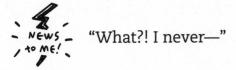 "What?! I never—"

"Pardon me for just a minute, girls." Mrs. Staughton is now standing. (Brooke mouths, "Thirty-four seconds.") "Whether you did—"

"I didn't!"

"I am not interested in who did what." She drops her clipboard on the table and glares at Heather. "Our mission is to provide food for individuals in need. No one in this room is in *need* of pizza. If we lose sight of our mission on our way to winning a contest, what does that make us?" She stares hard at us.

"Not winners. Now"—she picks up her clipboard—"how many of you spoke with your elderly pers—people?"

Everybody except Nora raises their hands. "Has anybody had a meeting?"

Faith and I keep our hands raised. "I have a question," Faith says. "If our elderly person gives us a list of things she wants in her basket, do we have to get them all?" Faith holds up the list. Mrs. Hallberg speaks with her privately.

"Meanwhile, we have a cornucopia of craft projects for your Thanksgiving baskets!" Mrs. Staughton visits each table. "Card making, bow tying, and turkey table toppers. Why don't you divide yourselves up and—" Everybody lunges for the turkey table topper table. "What about my card makers and bow tie-ers? Heather?"

TURKEY TABLE TOPPER featuring...

Hot glue gun ãnd googly eyes

* NOT actual sizes

Heather, Allie, and Faith switch to bow tying. Elsa sits down at the card table. "Want to get the cards out of the way?" Brooke asks. I glance over and Nora is hot-gluing her pinecone to her orange. Eliza is cutting a beak out of construction paper.

"I'll make cards with you, Brooke," Lily says before I have a chance to answer.

I sit down beside Nora. She is the first one finished with her topper. Eliza is second. And I lean mine against Eliza's.

"Mrs. Staughton, I'm afraid our toppers are . . . floppers," Mrs. H. observes.

"Hold on." Mrs. S. sets a half-finished bow down and rifles through her fanny pack. "Voy-la! Flopper-stoppers!" She empties a bag of O-shaped washers onto the table. "Hot-glue one of these to your bottoms—all your problems will be solved. And make sure to put your names on them so we can tell them apart." I hear Brooke snort, which makes me wish I was at the card-making table.

Since it's our last meeting before Thanksgiving, Mrs. Staughton asks us to share one thing Junior Guides has made us grateful for during our closing circle. I go first.

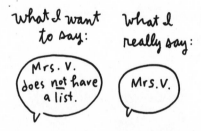

Nora goes last. Everybody is 150% expecting her to pass.

Mrs. Klein drives us home. Nora and I are quiet in the backseat, but I can still hear her say, "Friends."

"Are you going anywhere for Thanksgiving, Kate?" Mrs. Klein asks.

"We always have Thanksgiving"—actually we always have everything—"at our house. My sister is running in the Gobble-Wobble 5K. Are you around?"

"Mr. Klein wanted me to take the girls house hunting, but it's our last Thanksgiving on the East Coast for a while. I'm going to miss the seasons."

"Dinner, Kate!" my dad yells up, and I swear, Rocky is downstairs before my dad says the t in Kate.

"I made our tacos tonight," Fern, my taco twin, announces. Dad smiles and hands me a fork. She puts the olives on her fingertips and nibbles them off while we're waiting. When we're all finally in our seats, she says, "What's that big box doing there anyway?" Everyone looks at my dad. "Right there!" she says, pointing.

"The big box *did* something? I missed it." (Family deep sigh.) "All right . . ." He hands the box to Robin. "Eight or nine weeks ago, you made a commitment to 'do the thing you think you cannot do.' A week from tomorrow, by this time, you'll have done it! Your mother and I bought you something special for race day."

EVERYTHING
CROSSED

X ← hair

O, please make them
the same as Will's!

"Wow, thanks," Robin says, and shakes it like it is not obviously a shoe box.

"New sneak—" Mom cups her hand over Fern's blabbermouth.

Robin holds the left one up. It's electric blue with a Day-Glo orange sole and laces.

"I think your dad wants to be able to see you coming from a mile away." Mom laughs. "They should fit, but there are lots of choices, and we have plenty of time to exchange them."

Robin hesitates. "You would think so—except Grace was planning to get new shoes and she read that you need at least *three* weeks to break them in . . . but I LOVE these—thank you!"

GENIUS!

Robin offers to listen to my Town Hall speech after dinner.

I will join the forces of revolution, BUT I am <u>not</u> revolting. I mean I cannot revolt -- this project is revolting. I can't wait till it's over. No offense, Hannah.

"So are you going to vote for the Revolution?" Robin asks.

"Hannah hasn't made up her mind," I answer. "Did Grace *really* read that?"

"About the sneakers? We both did, but it was her idea to Google it in the first place. It's really three weeks if you're going to run a marathon, not a 5K—"

"But you're not going to wear Will's, either."

"I was thinking I might ask Will to return them." She lifts my jaw (which has dropped). "Kate, you saw Dad's face; no way I'm returning those."

"Maybe Will might give you something else. . . ."

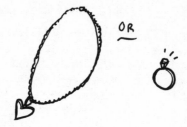

"Maybe. Hey, I have a ton of homework." (*Translation:* Good night.)

The LONG ~~DREADED~~ awaited TOWN MEETING

After recess, we change into our Town Meeting costumes. I'm wearing the same thing I wore for my Maryland colony presentation last month. Brooke (whose mother is an excellent seamstress) has a new imitation deerskin dress, shell necklace, and the best part: her old braids. I kind of want to hug her, but she only looks like Old Brooke. She's Onatah, and she's totally against the Revolution.

OYEZ, OYEZ! Hear ye, hear ye!

"As your Town Crier, it is my official duty to begin the meeting." Mrs. Block clangs her bell one last time, then sets it down. "Meeting begun. Now let me introduce your distinguished Moderator." She takes off her tricornered hat and coat, puts on a pair of glasses, and makes her voice gruffer. "Thank you, Town Crier, and good afternoon, fellow citizens. Whither the revolution? That is the question before

Which WITHER? with her? as in OR withers at base of horse's neck

175

us. May I humbly remind you that we have come together this afternoon as friends and good neighbors; let us vow to leave as such." Mrs. B. bangs a gavel on the desk. "Our first speaker, Rebecca West."

When it is time to vote, the forces of revolution seem to have it.

"All ye in favor of joining the forces of revolution—"

"Joining the forces or actually revolting—?" I ask with my yea hand wobbling under my chin.

OTHER OPTIONS?
1. NAYAY MAYBE
2. ABSTAIN ↰
(voting word
for "PASS")

"Vote yea or nay. One person, one vote. Hands raised high and say yea." Brooke, Peter, and Hui Zong are staring at my hand, waiting to see which way it will go.

"All ye opposed, raise your hands and say nay." Somebody-trick whinnies. I say nay. Mrs. B. counts twice. "Tie. All ye in favor of meeting again?"

(IT'S UNAYNIMOUS.)

NNN·A·y?!!!!

Mrs. B.'s hat is back on. She rings her bell. "As Town Crier, it is my official duty to close this meeting.

Meeting adjourned. Revolutionary identities adjourned! Let us snack and restore some unity to our community."

She unsnaps her ruffle collar. "As your *teacher,* it is my official duty to congratulate you on a job well done. You and I know, in the end, the forces of revolution won, but if you were living back then, it was not at all clear. As each of you adopted an identity and a point of view, you learned that 'history' has a point of view. And over time, many stories, little pieces of history, are lost, forgotten, or overlooked. Thank you for playing your role in history . . . and now off with your costumes so I can get you to the gym on time."

"I was surprised you didn't vote yea, you know, the winning side . . . ," Brooke says in the girls' bathroom.

"Guess that's the difference between me and Hannah." Brooke is taking out her braids. "I miss y—them." How embarrassing, I almost said "you."

Sometimes my MOUTH has a mind of its own.

Quiver · ONATAH'S Arrow

Brooke looks right at me and says, "Oh, let me guess why—you're not better than Eva at everything."

"Eva? I—"

"Don't get all upset. Like my mom said, I couldn't go through my whole life being 'Kate's best friend.' I have to figure out—"

"You mean Nora has to figure—"

"Nora has nothing to do with this."

"Or those?" I point to her glasses. "She has *everything* to do with it. You're—"

"*You're* making us late for gym, Kate," she says, and heads back to class.

HISTORIC FIRST · FIGHT with Brooke (not disagreement, misunderstanding, etc.)

I'm crying alone in the bathroom, like a stupid scene from a stupid movie.

MRS. V.'s BEST FRIEND

"That dog gets more of a greeting than I do," Dad says.

I'm about to say, "He gives more of a greeting," but when I look up, I see that my dad has clearly had a little too much late-afternoon time on his hands.

"How did Hannah do?"

"Ended up a tie."

"You make it sound like you lost." He removes the oat box. "Everything okay, Champ?"

If I tell him about Brooke, I'll start crying again. "Fine." I manage to half smile.

"You owe your grandmother an update." He holds out the phone. "C'mon, we're talking forty-six seconds of your precious time."

The phone rings right after I put it down. "Mrs. Geller?" There's a shaky voice on the other end.

"She's not home," I answer.

My dad starts to reach for the phone. "Is that you, Kate? This is Edie—Mrs. Verlangen. Verdi's missing! I hate to bother you—"

"It is one hundred percent not a bother, Mrs. Verlangen. I'll be right over." I hang up. "Mrs. V. can't find her cat," I tell my dad, grabbing my coat and running out the door.

"Call if you need help, Katie!" he yells after me.

I ring the bell, and Mrs. V.'s door flies open. She is already backing down the hall on her scooter. "You know Verdi's never missed tea—I haven't seen him since the last time you were here. Kate, I'm afraid he must've darted out when I opened the door."

"But he's so big, so white, I'm sure we would've—"

Giuseppe Verdi
(Translation: Joe Green)
Great Opera Composer
♪ 1813 - 1901 ♫

"Oh, Kate." She grabs my hands. "White, green-eyed cats are deaf—of course I didn't know when I named him. Verdi's spent his entire life indoors. I'm so afraid for him, and—"

She looks down and smooths her skirt.

"Mrs. Verlangen, you stay right here." DUHHHH. "I am going to find him." I step outside. It's hard to resist calling for him.

The Duh-bell

Duh "!" Duh
"where's she going to go?"

SUPER over-promise KATE to the rescue!

with super-size Verdi!

At first, I totally believe I'm going to find him. A big white cat will be easy to spot.

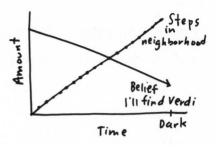

It's starting to get dark when I let myself back in. "No luck?" Mrs. V. calls down the hall. "I can tell by your shuffle."

"I'll put up some signs," I offer. "I just need a picture." Mrs. V.'s face falls. "Never mind, I'm good at cats."

It was pitch-black when I got back from putting up the signs. "Kate, your father has phoned twice—you best run home." I bend over to hug her, but Mrs. V. cups my face with her hands. "You are a best friend."

The wind blows my tears sideways, into my hair. My dad doesn't mention them when I walk into the kitchen.

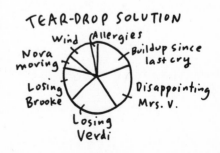

"Come here, Kate. I'm sorry I put an end to your search—it's dark, and dinner's waiting. I'll help you look after school tomorrow. Promise." He holds out his pinky.

"We *have* to find him, Dad. If you could see her—this is breaking her heart, I mean literally."

SUPER ~~Big~~ LITTLE SISTER

After school the next day, I flop my backpack and then myself on the kitchen floor.

"Long week, Champ?" Dad looks down at me. I close my eyes and hang my tongue out the side of my mouth. Rocky licks it.

BLYECH

"Let's find that cat," Dad says, pulling me up. We leave through the garage. "White with green eyes—is Verdi more of an extrovert or an introvert?—adventurous or shy?"

"Dad, I've been trying to get to know Mrs. Verlangen. I wasn't doing a personality test on her cat."

Halfway down our driveway, my dad starts calling Verdi.

"He's deaf, Dad."

"Right. That makes it harder, for sure." We traipse around the neighborhood until the sky is streaked, pink and purply-blue.

"Sorry, Champ," my dad says.

"It beats looking alone," I say.

"I think we earned a couple of flufferellas," he says, lining up the creamy peanut butter, marshmallow fluff, and Nutella on the counter. "Cats are survivors. Verdi—"

"Is a deaf indoor cat, Dad."

Things I inherited from my dad:

1. Hate to disappoint people (and Rocky)
2. Sweet tooth
3. I like to write.
4. Humor? (Please no.)

We finish our sandwiches in silence, and I excuse myself (just from the table, not for being mean) and go upstairs. Rocky is on my heels. He pushes Robin's door open. "C'mon, Rock, we're not supposed to go in there without permission." He is sitting next to Robin.

"Please, Kate, I'm trying to read."

I close the door as softly as I can, but then I have to reopen it. Rocky is scratching on the other side. "Sorry!"

Dinner is unusually quiet. Correction: Robin and I are unusually quiet, so our parents are unusually talkative. "How'd we do with Bob?"

> Never grow a wishbone, daughter, where your backbone ought to be.
> —Clementine Paddleford

Mom goes first. "Each of you girls has asked me whether I believe your wishes will come true, and I've given you the same answer: You have to make your wishes come true; you can't sit back and wait for someone else. I thought

Clementine
Paddleford
1898-1967

food writer,
pilot,
world traveler

Clementine said it better, and children generally hear things better coming from someone other than their parents."

"I wish I could find Verdi," I say. "I'm willing to do the work—to do whatever it takes to get him back."

My mom gives my forearm a little squeeze.

"You can have all my wishbones," Fern offers, and before I can thank her, she adds, "Trade for your Lego people."

"There's that backbone!" Dad laughs, glances at Robin (who hasn't even quarter-smiled all dinner), and passes Bob to Mom so she can pick.

The cure for boredom is curiosity.
There is no cure for curiosity.
—Dorothy Parker

IT ALSO
KILLED
the CAT.

Robin goes up to her room as soon as she finishes the dishes. "Kate," Mom says. "I don't want to put you in the middle—"

"Then you should've had me first instead of Robin—middle sister, get it?"

EXCELLENT ~~GOOD~~ ONE! (not to brag)

"Very funny. Do you know what's going on with your sister?"

Besides the Thing I'm not supposed to tell you?

"Never mind. Mrs. Klein called—she doesn't have to work this weekend, and Nora would like to invite you and Brooke over for a sleepover. Sounds like the three of you are getting along better."

That's because you didn't hear me crying earlier. I consider telling her the whole story, but she'll want to fix things. Instead I ask, "Did Brooke say yes?" Mom frowns. "Never mind, I'll go."

UNFIXABLE Situations:
1. Verdi
2. Brooke
3. Peter Buttrick

"Fern's out like a light,"* Dad says.

"I'm going to head up, then. 'Night." I tiptoe into my room and feel around under the bed for my book.

"Kate," Fern whispers.

*OUT LIKE a LIGHT -
O: The kind that goes on when you walk by.

"No, it's Clementine Paddleford. You are dreaming." I make my exit.

"Kate? Snuggle? Please?" You'd have to have a frozen flagpole for a backbone not to give in. I fold my knees behind hers on my third of her big-girl bed, and she's asleep half a minute later, so I slide out. "Kate?"

"Go to sleep, Fern."

I walk down to Robin's room. "Mind if I?" I hold up my book and lie on her other bed. "Are you and Grace running tomorrow?"

"Remember we're—" She holds up her book.

"Sorry." I open the book.

"Kate, you're sleeping. Your book fell on the floor ten minutes ago." She holds it out. "I have some news about Will. He isn't going to get me anything else."

Big Little sister,
come to me!

"Oh. That's—"

She has tears in her eyes. "I told him Mom and Dad got me the sneakers. He totally understood. Then he said he had something he needed to tell *me*." *Dum da dum dum* . . . "He really likes me, but he just wants to be friends."

I kneel on the bed so I am taller when I hug her. "He said it wouldn't change anything, the three of us would still hang out together, but it changes *everything*." She's wiping the tears with her palms, but I don't let go. "Grace is really mad at him." *Phew, someone else knows.*

MOM!
HELP
DAD!
Press
HERE!

"Me too." There must be something else I can say.

She gets back on her bed. "Don't worry. I'll be fine. I mean, it's definitely better for my training. Sorry, you can go to sleep now."

"Now? I'm wide awake."

"Well, read some more. It put you to sleep before."

FRIENDLY GHOST

"Morning, Sluggabed!" (*Translation:* Honorary name for last one out of bed in the morning. Root word = slug.) "Eva called. She wants you to come over with Robin and shoot some hoops."

A-wake: Yay, it's Saturday! B-wake: Boo, Verdi's still lost. "I want to find Verdi. And I have the sleepover at five."

"Better call Mom and let her know they don't have to come back for you. She took Robin shopping. I've got leftover pancakes." I swap my cereal bowl for a plate. "Something's up with your sister. . . ."

I don't disagree. I change the subject. "Dad, do you know where I could buy some lingonberry jam?"

"Ja, Sweden."

"Ja, not helpful. I was hoping to put Verdi in

HELLO,
The BREAK-
UP ?!!

CALLING all
POWERS in
the UNIVERSE

4-leaf
clovers

NECKLACE
CLASPS

EYE-
LASHES

wish-
bones

LUCKY
pennies

Birthday
candles

Mrs. Verlangen's Thanksgiving basket. And I want to find some good tea. Think you could show me how to make your pumpkin pie?"

"My baby-poo pie, as you so fondly refer to it."

"It's for Mrs. Verlangen. I want to make a practice one today."

CRUSTOLOGY

From the kitchen of DAD

2½ c. flour
1 tsp. salt
2 tbsp. sugar
3/4 c. (1½ sticks) butter, chilled
½ c. Crisco ← SECRET INGREDIENT
6-8 tbsp. ice water

Put 1½ c. flour, sugar, and salt in food processor or blender. Mix 5 seconds.

00:05

Then sprinkle butter and Crisco on top. Mix 15 secs. Sprinkle 1 c. flour on top. "Pulse" 5 times.

FLOUR

SCO

Sprinkle ice water on top. Mix till it forms dough.

Divide in two, wrap in plastic, flatten into disk. Refrigerate 1 hour. (Make cat toys.)

t.p. roll → fleece

Take out of fridge and let sit for 10 mins. before rolling out.

You may NOT want to sing ROLLING, ROLLING like Dad.

"Set the timer for forty minutes, Kate," my dad says as he closes the oven door. "Now let's find you some lingonberry jam." I follow him up to his office. "You've got your IKEA, and it looks like Fossinger's right here in town has some. They also have a purple tea infuser. I can run you over on the way to Nora's." He turns to face me. "Pie baking was *not* on my morning schedule. I need to get a few things done around the house." (*Translation:* You're on your own, kid.)

V ery
E asy to talk to
R ? ? ?
L aughs
A lot
N ever complains
G lad she is my
E lderly person and
N ew friend

I am stuck on the R when the phone rings. "Kate?" It's Brooke—too late to untake the call. "Nora told me that Mrs. Verlangen's cat is lost." She waits for me to say something. "Kate?"

"I'm listening."

"Teacake escapes all the time, and I'm the one who finds him."

"Your cat is not deaf."

"Kate? I'm sorry about what I said in the bathroom. You don't have to help me look. Let me do this for you—her. I need to get inside Mrs. V.'s house. Can you call her?"

"I guess so. I mean, okay. Just a second, please." I cover the phone. "Dad, can Brooke come over to help me find Verdi?"

"As long as I don't have to take you two anywhere—Is that the timer?" He skids into the kitchen after me and grabs the phone. "Brooke, Kate will call you right back."

"Dad?!" I shriek.

"You're going to make the pie fall." He sticks the thermometer back in the drawer. "Now you want to let it cool for a couple of hours." I nod; I'm on the phone again, waiting for Brooke to pick up.

"Hi, it's me," I say. "If your mom can drop you off, the two of us can look together."

I call Mrs. Verlangen while I wait for Brooke. She sounds like I woke her. "I'm afraid I'm not up for much today, dear."

"My friend Brooke is coming over—you don't need to entertain us or anything. Brooke's more of a cat person, and she thinks she can help us find Verdi. Apparently, most indoor cats never go more than a few houses away."

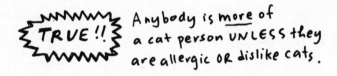

TRUE!! Anybody is more of a cat person UNLESS they are allergic OR dislike cats.

I meet Brooke in the driveway. Her mom waves. "So she doesn't think we'll be best friends forever?" I say as the car pulls away.

"No—I mean, yes. She just wants me to be my own person *and* your best friend."

"That's what I want, too."

"Duh," Brooke says, and runs toward Mrs. V.'s.

Brooke stands behind me when I ring the bell. "So, you're Brooke. You have beautiful hair and very interesting glasses. Come in." Mrs. Verlangen smiles and takes her hand.

I see Mrs. V. through Brooke's eyes, for a *second* first time, and she looks very small. Then my eyes are mine again, and I can see Mrs. V. trying to be cheerful. Brooke crouches down and looks under the little table by the piano.

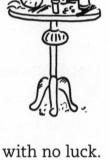

"I've searched everywhere," Mrs. V. says, scootering back to the kitchen. "But you girls are welcome to have a look around. What's a little mess among new friends?"

We spend twenty minutes downstairs with no luck. "We *have* to open drawers, Kate," Brooke insists. "Some cats sleep in open drawers and their owners shut them in by mistake."

"Not underwear drawers—"

"Every drawer. C'mon." The most interesting stuff (perfume bottles, little painted boxes, photographs, silver brushes, etc.) and the most private stuff (medicines, denture glue, foot bandages) are all sitting out, and we don't touch it.

"We're going upstairs!" Brooke calls.

"But she never goes upstairs," I argue.

"She's not the one who's missing." Brooke's already halfway up. She looks back. "Are you afraid?"

NoYesNoYes. "It's just that no one's been up there in a really long time." I follow her. The light switch doesn't work. "Want me to get a light—?"

Brooke opens the door. I scream as Verdi flashes past. "Wow, I've never seen you move that fast! It's Verdi, the friendly ghost!" Brooke laughs.

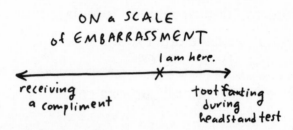

"Ah, *wunderbar!* Where are my Thanksgiving angels?!" Mrs. V. waits at the bottom of the stairs. Brooke and I are beaming.

"He was in the bedroom at the top of the stairs," Brooke says.

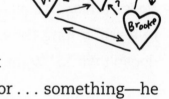

Mrs. V. shakes her head. "I sent the town nurse up there for, for . . . something—he must've followed her in there. Oh, I'm so relieved.

Reasons why Brooke
is my Best Friend:

15. She is an animal person.

16. She is good at finding things.

17.+ She found Verdi!
18.

Look at me crying—well, now you've seen it all, Kate! I wish I had a reward for you girls."

"I'd like to try some lingonberry jam," Brooke says.

"Kate's told you about that, has she?" We're all still smiling.

sNORA's FIRST SLEEPOVER

"Nora's in the basement, girls."

Personally, I've never been in the Kleins' basement. Meanwhile, Brooke goes running down the hall. I'm afraid I'm losing her again.

"Follow Brooke," Mrs. Klein says. "Nora's dragged all of creation down there, but if there's anything you need, I'm packing up the kitchen, right in here."

"Thanks, Mrs. Klein!"

"Did you bring your K8 ball?" Nora greets me.

"Snap. You should've reminded me. You have Ping-Pong?!" Not to brag, but Ping-Pong is my best sport.

"You two play," Nora says. "Winner stays."

I beat Brooke, and she gives Nora the paddle. "I'm going to the bathroom."

"Okay," Nora says. "Loser stays." *Wha—?*

what I think:

(Loser changes
the rules.)

what I say:

(Rally for
serve.)

I go to the bathroom after I beat Nora. "Hey, Nora, what's this?"

"A bathroom?" Play stops and she looks over. "Oh, that. That is a freaky embarrassment. Please close the door and forget you ever saw it."

"But there have to be a thousand cans in there!" Brooke exclaims.

"Welcome to my mom's disaster-preparedness

pantry—you know, in case of an alien takeover, World War III, stormzilla—wait, where are you going?"

Our LADY of the CANS

"Mrs. Klein?!" Brooke and I race into the kitchen. "You aren't going to move all those cans to California, are you?" I ask.

"Geez, girls, I have not given the basement a single thought. No, I suppose I—"

"Our canned food drive!" Brooke exclaims. And we both add, "Pleeeeeeease?"

"I don't know where my brain's been," she says, stepping down off her ladder. "Of course! If you girls pack them up and load them into my car, they're yours!"

"But what if there's a disaster, not counting ruining my first sleepover . . . ," Nora grumbles. I know just the thing to persuade Nora.

We load the last case of cans into the car and flop down on our sleeping bags. "Let's just sleep in our clothes and get right to the movie!" Nora says. "I call *Star Trek*—Look, I did what you two wanted for the last three hours; it's my turn. Besides, it's my first sleepover—could be my last . . ."

"Jiffy Pop, girls?" Mrs. Klein offers from the top of the stairs.

Nora translates: "Popcorn. It's pretty cool if you haven't seen it before. Puffs up like a genie hat."

Mrs. K. makes each of us our own. "Thank you for helping me clear out my pantry!" she says, and sends us downstairs.

Four minutes later, Nora is asleep with her hand in the Jiffy Pop. Brooke and I are "alone."

"Thanks again, a duodecillion times, for finding Verdi."

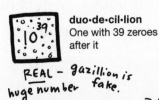

duo·de·cil·lion
One with 39 zeroes after it

REAL - gazillion is huge number fake.

"Sure." She takes Nora's hand out of her Jiffy Pop and offers me some. "My elderly person is nice, I guess, but we mostly talked about how she couldn't hear me because she's wasn't wearing her hearing aids. I wish we were still going to the nursing home. . . . You're better at change. My mom wants me to 'embrace' change. The hair and glasses thing was mostly her idea."

EMBRACE CHANGE:

HUG A QUARTER.

"Oh, no, I'm worse at change. If I had helped you pick the glasses, you'd still be wearing your old ones. But I'm used to—I mean, I *like* the new ones now."

She puts her glasses on the table and turns off the light. I fall asleep while we're talking.

"sNORA"

"Brooke's mom is here!" Mrs. Klein calls down early Sunday morning.

"That's a first," Nora says. "What about my going-away quilt?" (Not shown: Blood from needle-pricks)

"Honey, that'll have to wait, or the girls can work on it at home and send you their squares."

After Brooke leaves, I help Nora bring stuff upstairs until my mom arrives. "We'll have to see if we can squeeze in another one of these before the holidays," she says to Mrs. Klein. "And please take me up on my offer—you can drop Nora at our place—she's welcome anytime."

Robin is in the front seat with her new blue-and-Day-Glo-orange feet up on the dash. "You breaking them in?" I ask.

"Got my fastest time. Three miles, twenty-six and a half minutes." She seems like her regular self.

"Was Will—?" I start to say, but Mom is opening her door. "Uh, so, will you be racing in them?"

"They seem to be *working*," she says. *Translation:* Will was working?

I get the rest of the story before bed. "Grace interrogated him— you have to officially swear not to tell. He still likes me, but he

in·ter·ro·gate
Ask a lot of questions (especially of a suspect)

(question-storm)

doesn't want us to be a secret. He's planning to ask me out on race day. Now, where's that book you were reading? Maybe it'll put *me* to sleep." She hugs me, and I turn to go. "Hey, how are things with Brooke?"

"Much better. Not like you and your ol' BFF, Alexandra—"

"Olivia."

"Yeah, anyway, I'm pretty sure Brooke and I will always be friends."

The COLOR GREEN

Dear Diary,

Today Brooke made library extra special.

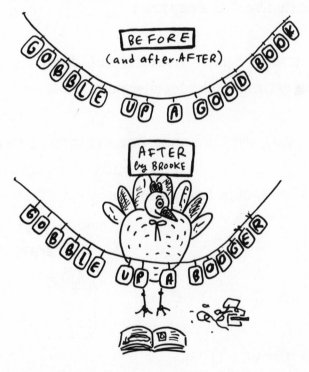

"I have basketball," I remind Brooke as we're packing up for dismissal.

"Eva must be absent; she's not in her waiting spot," Brooke says while we're walking down the hall.

"She probably already went to the gym," I say, wishing I could tell Brooke everything—about Robin, Will, Eva, and me. "See you tomorrow!"

Eva and I get to the gym at the same time. "I think it's officially over," she says.

"Yeah, I know," I say. Obviously she doesn't know about the getting-back-together part.

"Ms. Crowley says it's not one hundred percent official, but 5C won the pizza party. Frankly, Nora won. She brought in twenty-one bags—"

"Today?"

As in OUR 21 BAGS from the NEIGHBORHOOD?

"A long time ago."

"Those were our—" That's really between me and Nora. "Never mind."

Coach Vic blows his whistle. "Bring it in! Coach Vic is ready to get started." We run three warm-up laps and I hide in the back row for foot fire. At the last minute, Eva shuffles down beside me.

"No offense, I know you're a Junior Guide," she half yells to be heard over the feet. "But everyone is actually sick of that canned food drive."

"I wasn't talking about the food drive. I was talking about—" The stampede stops right when I half yell, "ROBIN AND WILL!"

"Robin and Will—please share!" Coach Vic folds his arms. "Coach Vic has you for practice ninety—9-0—minutes this week. You have the other nine thousand, nine hundred, and ninety to discuss Robin and Will. Again!"

Coach Vic shows us a new play. "Coach Vic calls this one G-R-E-E-N." He draws it on his clipboard. "Sammi brings the ball up and yells, 'Green!' You two cut to the corners. Erin

COACH VIC'S CLIP BOARD

(I am GREEN with DRY-ERASE envy.)

sets a pick on Kate's defender. Sammi—WOOP!—passes the ball to Kate. Kate fakes, shoots, scores!" He looks up. "We are going to make sure our fifth graders—our 'green' players—get plenty of chances to S-C-O-R-E, because—let the fifth graders answer, please: Are winners the ones who score the most? Listen carefully to Coach Vic—winners are the ones who contribute the most to the S-U-C-C-E-S-S of the team. Get up! Let's run it!"

After practice, Eva and I are changing back into our regular clothes. "You know," she says (I *do* know, but I'll let her tell me), "my brother and your sister are still friends and everything."

Robin-Will
KNOWLEDGE

hers

mine

KATE the > EVA!

"I know," I say.

Didst thou listen deeply to Coach Vic?

Pepto Dismal

My backpack lands with a thud on the seat next to Nora.

"What do you have in there?" she asks.

"Cans—for the pep rally. Not twenty-one bagsful or anything . . ." Nora turns back to the window. "I thought your mom gave our cans to Mrs. Staughton."

"I can't help what you thought. Ms. Crowley had to store the bags until the Guide meeting. Then when the pizza contest started, Ms. C. pointed out that it would be just as easy to have the homeroom turn them in, and I didn't see why not."

"Because HALF of them belonged to me, that's why. Not. And you could've said something at the Guides meeting. Whatever happened to 'We tell each other everything'?"

"Like I ever say *anything* at the Guides meeting. You can take your half of the cans. I didn't know you needed to win the pizza party, too."

Silence. I don't *need* to win a pizza party. I *need* a friend I can trust.

"Whatever," Nora goes on. "And you can have the cans from my mom's pantry. I'm used to being a loser." I'm looking out the other side of the bus, but I can see her rub her eyes.

CRYING IS my KRYPTONITE.

I don't need to make her cry. Besides, I forgot about the pantry.

Brooke's holding up her backpack when we get off the bus. "Feel this!"

"Feel *this*!" I say. The backpacks weigh the same, but we each practically tip over trying on the other one's. "News flash: Nora's homeroom won," I say.

THE KLEINS' 1,000-CAN CAR

"It's not over—"

"Her mom's pantry?"

"Oh, yeah," Brooke says. "Then I'm giving my cans to the pep rally. I want to see the cancan."

"What is a cancan?" Nora asks.

"Shuball wube dubance?"

Farley's rallies are low on pep. We don't have a football team, or cheerleaders, or a marching band.

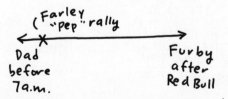

We just have a principal who used to be a football player, and everybody else (kids and teachers included) is happy about any excuse to get out of class the day before Thanksgiving vacation.

Mr. Mac is at the mike. "Mr. Lovejoy has another, uh, obligation, so I am going to get things rolling here this morning. A big congratulations to Farley's Pod 429, Pack 22, and the rest of you for collecting a record number of cans. Give yourselves a round of applause. And will Ms. Crowley's homeroom please come forward?

"You're looking at the pizza party winners—these fifth graders collected five hundred twelve cans." He claps into his microphone, and the rest of the clapping immediately stops so people can cover their ears.

The cancan music comes on, and Nora and her class are stuck standing up there.

"Friends, the BIGGEST"—Mr. Lovejoy is out of breath—"WINNER (breath) HERE (breath) is . . . Kynlyn's Barley Sheaf Pantry." He motions to their truck, which is parked on the outdoor basketball court. "They will be driving away with more than twenty-five hundred cans." He yells "GO!" into the microphone, then holds it out and the crowd (except the seventh and eighth graders, who are too cool) yells "CAMELS!" And in trots the Farley Fighting Camel.

The Fighting Camel almost falls when the FRONT fixes her fanny pack.

Mr. Lovejoy has his arm around the truck driver from the food pantry. "My friends from Barley Sheaf tell me they have packed up forty-seven hundred pounds of food, which will enable them to serve over forty-three hundred meals! And, Nora, don't you go anywhere—do you recognize this person? Please give a warm Farley welcome to Nora's mom, Mrs. Klein. She just dropped off another thousand-odd cans. This mother-daughter team are Farley's fourth annual Harvest Food Drive heroes. . . . Can I call you heroes, heroines?" Microphone clap.

"One last congratulations to Ms. Crowley's homeroom . . . and to the members of Pod 429 and Pack 22, who will be celebrating this Saturday at Luau Keys. And happy Thanksgiving to all my Farley friends. We have so much to be grateful for."

Frankly, All Farley friends
are grateful for the following:

1. NO homework
2. No word of the week
3. Bus break (No offense, Gene.)
4. Private bathrooms

"I saved you some." Nora hands me a pizza slice wrapped in greasy napkins, on the bus.

"Thanks. Are you helping with the baskets tomorrow?"

She shakes her head. "I don't have an elderly person, and my mom's making a huge deal about our last Thanksgiving here."

I let Nora past when we get to her stop. "See you Saturday," she says.

"You're coming to Luau Keys?!" I ask, but Gene has already closed the door.

THANKSGIVING EVE DAY

My mom and Robin are crumbling cornbread for stuffing, and Fern is taking the ends off the string beans. (My old job.) "Eighty-four baskets!" my dad says. "Marion Staughton had to call in Pack 22 to help. Yours truly was Junior Bird Man."

"Dad helped Mr. Hallberg with the turkeys," I explain.

My dad swipes a string bean. "Always guard your pot, Fern-o. Speaking of which, you better put Mrs. Verlangen's basket up where Mr. Voracious can't get at it, Kate."

vo·ra·cious
Hungry with 39 zeroes after it

aka Mr.V.

"Those aren't instant potatoes. . . ." My mom's instant radar has detected the weakest item in my gift basket. "I'll send you over with some real mashed potatoes tomorrow." She rests her hands on the stuffing pan. "What do you think about having Mrs. Verlangen for Thanksgiving dinner?"

"Turkey is more traditional," my dad says. Mom throws a piece of cornbread at him. "Is Lois going to be okay with that?" Dad asks.

"We had plenty of company at Thanksgiving while I was growing up. . . . You know my mother, she'll be . . . herself. Kate?"

"I don't think she'll come, but sure, I'll ask her. I'm going to make a PB and J, then I'll walk over."

"Make that two, please," Fern says, which is how I end up making five.

"Kate! I wasn't expecting you until later!" Mrs. Verlangen swings the door shut. She opens it again. "Take two: Kate! How nice to see you. Won't you come in? Now, would you mind waiting a minute while I finish what I was doing?" She scoots down the hall.

I study the photographs on the wall while I'm waiting. "Is that your daughter?" I ask her when she gets back.

"Yes. That's Lida, taken in California a long time ago. Have you been?"

"That's where Nora is moving."

"Well, it's a very nice place to visit," she says, and heads toward the kitchen.

"Just a sec, I have to grab my— your—basket."

I set it on her lap. "All of this is for me?" She runs her hand over the cellophane.

"And Verdi."

"I'll show him at teatime. It's so pretty, Kate, I hate to ruin it." She wears the purple bow as a headband. "One does not need a great deal of money to feel rich," she says as she takes the card out of the envelope. She sets the lingonberry

jam on her lap, then admires her basket again. "Now, what is this? Ready-to-bake—it looks homemade."

"We're going to make it together."

"Kate, it's been, oh . . . at least fifteen years since I baked a pie."

"It's been four days since I baked my very first."

She's already cleared a space and emptied the box onto the table. "See if my apron is still hanging in that broom closet, would you, dear?" She catches herself and adds, "Please! Now, put that butter in the freezer and take the blue ceramic bowl down. My pastry cutter is in the drawer to the right of the sink."

Mrs. V. cuts the butter into the dry ingredients. "Ice water? Thank you." She closes her eyes and smells the dough. "I like to knead it a touch—Verdi, scat! Shoo, cat!" She waves her dish towel at Verdi, who has parked himself in the cleared spot. He stretches, then saunters over to the edge of the table and jumps.

oh yum, CAT HAIR PIE!

"It's a good thing he's deaf, or I'd be forced to think he doesn't listen. Hand me a sponge, dear." She pours the crumbly dough onto some waxed paper. "Like this—take a little bit and smear it away from you, with the fingers—the heels are too warm. Now you do the rest." I make the smears into a ball and wrap it in the waxed paper. Mrs. V. says, "I have been known to freeze my dough—I've never been known for my patience." She laughs. "But I suppose we're in no hurry."

I wash the blue bowl and sit down. "Kate, I have a small something for you." I see two somethings wrapped in a pillowcase on the table.

CARDS GO → HERE

LOOK CARDS

side view

F.EYE too-small hand

LOOK THROUGH HERE

STEREOSCOPE and CARDS ↑

"These were my grandmother's, Oma Inge. The town nurse brought them down from Lida's room when she accidentally shut my little friend in." Verdi is back on her lap. "I'm afraid I'm not much of a shopper anymore. Shall I show you?" She sits a card on the little easel and holds the glasses up so I can look through. The pictures on the two cards become one.

"I love it," I say.

She hands me the stereoscope. "That was Mozart's home. A lot of the cards are from Austria, but I've kept the collection up over the years. Mr. Verlangen would always bring me new ones from his travels."

"I'll store them here so you—"

"No, no, take them home and show Fern. And Robin. And Brooke. Even Nora. If I miss them, I'll know where to find them." She turns the oven on. "Four hundred?" She has me get her walker so she can stand to roll out the dough, and she teaches me how to crimp the edges of the crust between my thumbs.

We mix the filling while the crust is baking, and when it's time, Mrs. V. lets me take the crust out *and* pour the custard in *and* put the pie back in the hot oven.

"Leave me a slice and take the rest home with you," Mrs. V. says as the pie cools.

"I was thinking, you could have Thanksgiving dinner at our house tomorrow and bring the pie with you."

"Is that what you were thinking?" She dabs her eye with her apron and gets pumpkin on her cheek. "Oh, help me off with this thing!" I take the apron. "There are just three problems with your thinking: one, you can't go around inviting neighbors to your Thanksgiving dinner." She waggles two fingers. "I've had a big day, and I can't tell you what kind of company I'll be tomorrow. And three, I fully intend to sample this pie before you leave."

"But you're not busy, are you? The invitation was actually my mom's idea."

"I have a date with my basket," she says, and sets two plates and forks out. "You do the honors." She hands me a knife.

227

PRE·RACE GRACES

Our house is all lit up, and the kitchen windows are steamy.

IMAGINATION $\gtreqqless$ REALITY!

It's the kind of house I'd pick for my HOME (if it wasn't already).

"How'd it go, Champ?" my dad says before I take off my coat.

"She won't know until tomorrow. She might be too tired."

"The pie. How was your pie?"

Kate, how about a tinch more?

"It was great, Dad."

HOW OUR PIE WAS...
(on my PIE SCALE of GREATITUDE)

BABY POO	X	LEMON MERINGUE (my FAVE)

"That's some magic kitchen—drinkable tea, great baby-poo pie. . . ."

I totally forgot the magic pillowcase I am holding. "Wait'll you see what she gave me! It was her grandmother's, and these cards are from all over the world."

"Wow, I've only ever seen these in antique shops." My dad is in love.

"What? What is it?" Fern and Rocky come bounding into the kitchen.

"It's an adult toy," my dad says, holding it out of Fern's reach.

ahem
(nobody
we know)
a dolt

a·dult Grown-up (not to be confused with a dolt = a stupid person)

"What's a dolt?" Fern asks.

"C'mon, Fern, Mrs. Verlangen wants you to see this." We view the cards through the stereoscope until my dad calls us to the table.

"We don't usually say grace, but tomorrow is unusual—it is Robin's first race. And for this special occasion, I have composed a pre-race grace." Dad holds his paper over the candle.

229

"Adam, you need your glasses. That's going to—" The paper catches fire, and my dad dunks it in his water glass.

"I have it memorized:

Dad's PRE-RACE MEAL
peas
Angel hair pasta with potatoes
salad

"May the angels who gave up their hair for the meal we are about to receive watch over you. May you run with Grace at your own pace. May you feel winnish at the finish. And now, let us din-nish."

"Maybe it's more of a toast." He raises his soggy paper water glass and we all clink 'n' drink.

"So, are you ready, Rube?" my dad asks, twirling his pasta, which inspires Fern to twirl her pasta.

"All I need now is a good night's sleep. I have some pre-race jitters, not like I'm going to win or anything—just my first race, I guess."

"How about I run you a bath and you can soak in the tub after dinner?" Mom says.

"I'll do the dishes," I offer.

"You can use my bath toys," Fern adds.

"That would be nice," Robin says.

I peek in Robin's room on my way to bed. She is asleep. Her book looks like a little tent pitched under her chin. I mark the place and stack it on her nightstand. She stirs when I turn out the light. "I was just resting."

"Don't forget Trolly," I say. He's her good-luck troll. I put him on top of her bag.

"Hey, Kay." She only calls me that when she's really tired. "I hope Will hasn't changed his mind." She sits up. "Would you do that egg thing on top of my head? That always helps me fall asleep."

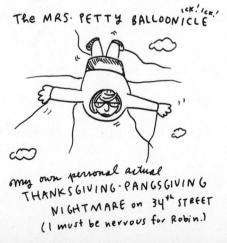

The MRS. PETTY BALLOONICLE ICK! ICK!

my own personal actual THANKSGIVING-PANGSGIVING NIGHTMARE on 34ᵗʰ STREET (I must be nervous for Robin.)

GOBBLY WOBBLY

Mom and Fern are making race posters at the kitchen table. Dad took Robin, and he's going to see the start, then book to the finish line so we can all be together. I grab a pumpkin muffin for the ride.

It's so crowded Mom has to park a few blocks away from the finish line. "Kate!" I hear my name before I'm out of the car.

"Who's that, Kate?" Mom asks.

"Eva, you know, Grace's sister. And her brother, Will." They're waving from across the street. Any thoughts of crossing are run over by the police car with the flashing lights, followed by the wheelchair racers.

EVERY ONCE in a LONG WHILE,

Mom decides NOT to explain.

"I want to try that," Fern says as they go sailing by.

232

The first runners show up forty-six seconds later. Then there's a steady stream. "I hope your dad makes it in time."

I hear his whistle before I see him. "Mom, he's over there with the Paysons."

"I'll see him later—Look! Here comes your sister!" Robin and Grace are holding hands. (And, please destroy after reading: I am crying for NO reason.) They raise their arms as they cross the finish line.

Will's the first one to hug Robin after they're done hugging each other. My dad's second. Mr. Payson is making a video.

My dad pulls a sweatshirt out of Robin's bag and hands it to her. "My car's right down here, Rob."

Grace hugs Robin goodbye and says, "I can't believe it's over. I know I was a real pain a lot of the time— I'll never be a jockette like you, but I'm really going to miss training."

"You don't *have* to stop," Robin says.

The second Geller Thanksgiving breakfast is served in front of the TV: apple pancakes and Thanksgiving parade with a side of bacon. My dad mutes the TV for a commercial.

"I noticed a certain Will Payson got the first hug." Now I'm looking for my dad's mute button OR my vaporizing spray.

"He seems very nice," Mom says. "Is he in tenth grade?" Okay, now I'm seeing Robin's point.

SISTER·DOUBLE!

"Yeah, he's really great." Robin hesitates. "He asked me to the Homecoming dance."

"PARADE'S BACK ON!" Fern and I double-shout. (Toni Morrison couldn't possibly have been talking about me and Fern.)

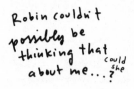

Next commercial, Mom picks up where she left off. "Homecoming *this* year?"

"Saturday night."

"Can you please have your dolt conversation later?" Fern can't hear and now I can't see because she's standing right in front of the TV.

"Look at the time!" Dad says. (*Translation:* Must leave room. Now.) "I better go stuff the bird."

"Let me take the stuffing out for you," Mom says. (*Translation:* May I have a word with you in the kitchen?)

"Robin, your mother and I could use a little assistance here." (*Translation:* See above.)

Mrs. Verlangen doesn't answer her phone when I call her at one o'clock. The same thing happens at three. "Give her one last try after Grammalolo gets here," Mom suggests. "Why don't you and Fern go throw the football around? Please keep her away from the leaf pile."

"APPROPRIATE"
Thanksgiving outfit

nice top

nice sports pants

skirt with leggings or tights ←0 chance 2 waistbands

my idea | mom's idea

Fern sees Grammalolo's car pull in. She spikes the football and runs over to meet her. "Easy now, don't tackle me." Grammalolo bends down to kiss Fern. "Hello, Snickelfritz. Take these for me—I brought my sweet potatoes, in case your mother is experimenting with hers again this year."

I run up and drop the pan on the only open counter space in the kitchen. "I'm going to bike over to Mrs. Verlangen's."

There's no answer when I ring Mrs. Verlangen's bell. I twist the knob, just in case. Then I knock and put my ear to the door. There's opera music, blaring louder than nine hundred of the world's loudest doorbells. I wait for a break in the music and ring again. And a third time. I straddle my bike (I do *not* peek in a single window) and push off. I hear, "Kate?"

"Grammalolo just got here. Are you coming?"

She looks down at her robe. "Can this pass for loungewear?" It kind of looks like a Japanese kimono. "Let me get a necklace. It would all go much faster if you fetched me my scooter."

"Can I ride it?"

> I.O.U.
> ~~~~~~~
> ONE
> SCOOTER LESSON
> Signed, Mrs V.

She actually thinks about it. "Next time. I'll give you a lesson."

Mrs. V. comes back wearing her necklace, bracelet, earrings, and fancy slippers. "Let's go." I don't want her to change her mind. She is staring at me. Major planning problem: Neither of us has figured out how she is actually going to get there. "Can you?" I look at the scooter.

"People do . . . all the time." She looks straight ahead nervously.

"Wear this." She refuses my helmet. "Wait, let me bike home. I'll get one of my parents."

"Too much bother. Go get the rest of our pie and lock the door behind you." Mrs. V. motors down the driveway.

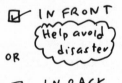

WHITHER · WHETHER
to RIDE . . .

☑ IN FRONT
(Help avoid disaster)

OR

☐ IN BACK
(witness disaster)

I bike in front. Every few seconds, I call out, "You okay?"

She never gives the same answer twice. "Splendid, Kate." "Better than the bee's knees." "Faster!"

A car slows down ahead of us, and the driver opens the window. "You two should have lights."

I turn toward Mrs. V. to say, "It's just my dad," and the pie slides off my handlebars.

"Can't cry over mashed pie!" she yells over the sound of her motor. "Ach, I hate to arrive empty-handed." She waves to my dad. "Mr. Geller, I'm Edie Verlangen. We'll make proper introductions at the house."

My dad helps Mrs. V. and her scooter through the garage and into the house. I lead her into the living room. Grammalolo stands and says, "Please, have my seat, or do you sit on *that*—?"

"Edie, I'm Kate's mom, Nancy Geller. Tell me, where will you be most comfortable?"

COMPASS of COMFORTABLENESS

N — Grammalolo

S

Grammalolo — Comfort

"It's all lovely," she says. Mrs. V. uses the handlebars to hoist herself up and onto the other end of Grammalolo's sofa. "Kate, can you park that for me?"

"Mrs. Verlangen, these are my sisters: Robin—"

"Aren't you pretty." It's the opposite of a question when Mrs. V. says it.

"And Fern." She stretches out her arms and Fern climbs into her lap so she can touch all the sparkles.

"What is that?" Grammalolo asks.

"These are Austrian glass beads." Mrs. Verlangen leans toward Grammalolo so she can take a closer look.

"No, I mean—" Grammalolo removes something from Mrs. V.'s robe.

"Oh, *that* is a piece of the most delicious pie you will never have the pleasure of tasting. Your granddaughter and I made it yesterday. Unfortunately, I ran over it on our way here." It already seems funny.

"To the table!" my dad calls from the kitchen.

I bring Mrs. V.'s scooter around. "I'm going to put you next to me, on the other side of Kate," Mom says.

whee!

Mrs. Verlangen is resting on her knuckles, getting ready to sit. The candles are flickering in her eyes. "Thank you for inviting me to your table."

"Long overdue," Dad says, and raises his glass. "Happy Thanksgiving, all!"

BACKWARDS* T3JJUB STYLE

*(Food moves. People stay put.)

"I know I say this every year, but—" my mom starts, and we all join in, "I can't believe it's already over." Mrs. Verlangen laughs.

"Not so fast—we still have pie!" my dad says. "You'll have to settle for *my* pumpkin, pecan, and I can serve it to you with vanilla ice cream or whipped cream or both!"

PUMPKIN   PECAN   sliver of BOTH   NEITHER

Robin and I stand up to clear. Grammalolo reaches for Mrs. V.'s plate. "You stay seated, dear."

"Just to warn you, Mrs. V.," Robin says. "Our dad is going to ask all of us what we're grateful for after we finish dessert."

"Good heavens, please tell me he is not going to do *that* again." Grammalolo sighs and rolls her eyes.

THANKSGELLERING

"Adam, it's getting late." My mom tilts her head in Mrs. Verlangen's direction. Her eyelids are drooping. "You should run Mrs. Verlangen home."

Mrs. Verlangen collects good-night kisses from my mom and my sisters, and I walk her out to the kitchen. "Thank you for coming."

"Thank you for coming into my world, Kate Geller."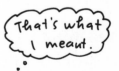

LUWOWZA KEYS

The pod is standing by the "ocean" pool. "It's not even salt water," Peter Buttrick announces, then does a cannonball into the waves.

#1 WATER PARK HOTEL

Nora finds a chair under a bamboo umbrella, as far as possible from the pool, and opens her book. We stow our stuff under her table. "Did you bring a bathing suit?" Brooke asks. Nora pulls a strap out from under her shirt.

"Lunch is at twelve-fifteen," Nora says, setting the schedule down and studying the ocean pool. "I think *that's* the one that gave my sister her rash."

Eliza walks up. "Want to do Paradise Falls?"

"Pirate Cruise! Please?" Brooke begs. (This is her fifth time.)

"As long you don't mind all the boys—that's what they're doing."

"How about the Mangrove Float?" Nora reads the description. "A relaxing—"

↖ KILLS IT

Brooke, Eliza, and I agree on Paradise Falls. "Sure you don't want to come, Nora?" I offer. She doesn't look up from her book.

AAAAAAHHH!

PARADISE FALLS!

Mr. Landry makes the lunch announcements: "Listen up: Everybody back here at four p.m. for afternoon snack. We'll do a group shot in the pool at four-fifteen, and your rides will be here at four-thirty. Bathrooms are located near the attraction entrances. Fair warning: every pool has been chemically treated with Wee Alert!"

"Hurricane Alley?" Eliza asks.

"We promised Nora we'd do the Mangrove Float. Meet you at Pirate Cruise after that?" Eliza heads off to Hurricane Alley.

"This is kind of boring," Nora says after we've been floating for approximately forty-five seconds. "I was thinking the rash could have been Wee Alert–related." She takes a ziplock bag full of snacks from her life vest.

"I don't think you're supposed to eat—"

"NO!" I hear Brooke yell, and I see her tube flip just before mine goes.

"Careful, the crocodiles are wild around here!" Josh Weiden says, then jumps back in his tube and paddles off.

"They have video surveillance," Nora says, crumpling her chip bag and putting it back in her vest.

Nora goes back to being our trip adviser for the remainder of the afternoon.

At picture time, Peter Buttrick is the first one in the ocean pool. "Peter!" Mr. Landry gasps.

"Wee Alert, Wee Alert!" Allie shouts. You can see the bright red plume from our bamboo table.

"Pixy Stix," Nora whispers.

Brooke uncovers her mouth. "Really?"

"Very funny," Peter says. The plume follows him to the side of the pool. "Seriously, it's Jell-O or something—cherry-flavored." He takes a big gulp of the water for proof.

"Peter, you will get sick from drinking that—that—" Mrs. Staughton stammers. "Out of the pool!"

"You? Pixy Stix? Peter?" Brooke looks at Nora admiringly. "In the snack line?" Nora nods. "Genius!" Brooke high-fives Nora. "I can't believe you could keep it a secret!"

GENIUS

"It's easy. I'm not used to having someone to tell . . . I better get unused to it," she says. "It's really weird to think I won't be here next Thanksgiving."

"Neither will we," I say, even though it's not the same. "No Junior Guides, no food drive . . ."

"I don't know. It's even weirder that you *are* here," Brooke says.

It is weird—the three of us sitting here—Nora at Rash City, Brooke in her new hair. I actually think I might have changed the most.

But maybe it's not supposed to be a contest.

The end is where we start from.
—T.S. Eliot

ACKNOWLEDGMENTS

Great big thanks to Kate's early readers and guest calligraphers (Brooke James, Kathy McCullough, Audrey Swartz, Gretchen Swartz, Madeline Toth, Lorene Jean, and Aurora Becker), my agent Edite Kroll, editor Phoebe Yeh, book designer Cia Boynton, art director Ken Crossland, Elizabeth Stranahan, and the rest of the team at Crown Books for Young Readers.

ABOUT the AUTHOR·ILLUSTRATOR

 Like Kate, Suzy Becker is a middle sister. She used to play the flute. She still loves to ride her bike, and she has a best friend named Brooke. *Kate the Great: Winner Takes All* is her eleventh book. Suzy and her family live in an old yellow farmhouse in central Massachusetts.

There's more GREATITUDE...

mrs. Petty
(The Art Teacher)

#2 I am very good at drawing. Except realistically. (Never mind Mrs. Petty.)

I am so a good boy.

My Dog, Rocky

#5 I am a really good sister. Except when I'm not.

#11 Dogs and little kids love me.

Will I survive Mrs. Petty; my big sister, Robin; and my frenemy, Nora?

(obviously, since I wrote all this.)

(No comment)

Find out the whole story!

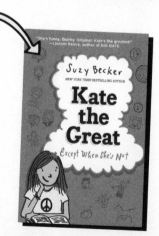

"She's funny. Quirky. Original. Kate's the greatest!"
—Lincoln Peirce, author of BIG NATE

SUZY Becker
NEW YORK TIMES BESTSELLING AUTHOR
Kate the Great
Except When She's Not

"May Kate continue to be this great!"
—The Horn Book

A Bank Street College of Education Best Children's Book of the Year